Twenty Hillcrest Road

B.W. Balser

Cold Tree Press
Nashville, Tennessee

Library of Congress Control Number: 2007922460

Published in the United States by Cold Tree Press
Nashville, Tennessee
www.coldtreepress.com

Printed in the United States of America
ISBN 978-1-58385-163-0

In this delightful book, the author has managed to convey how it felt to grow up in a small New England town in the fifties. It is told from the viewpoint of Ben, the middle son of a traditional family where mom stays home and dad is the breadwinner. The relationship with his parents and grandfather, schoolboy angst and first love are told with frankness and a spirit of adventure. The reader can't help but sympathize with the plight of the young narrator as he relates the trials and tribulations of childhood.

—Fran Hegarty, Technical Services
Peabody Institute Library
Danvers, Massachusetts

Mr. Balser writes well and the story moves along and is believable.

—Rosemary Kingsland
best-selling British author of
The Secret Life of a Schoolgirl

To Josiah Wentworth (1874-1967), my grandfather,
the most important person in my life.

ACKNOWLEDGEMENTS

There are several individuals who were instrumental in the production of TWENTY HILLCREST ROAD.

First, I want to point out that without the publishing expertise and professionalism of Peter Honsberger of Cold Tree Press none of this would have come to fruition. It was a delightful experience! I will always consider him a friend and look forward to publishing more books with him.

Director Douglas Rendell and his staff at the Peabody Institute Library in Danvers, MA, were invaluable (and patient!) in teaching me the necessary computer skills.
They include: Donna Maturi, Jennifer McGeorge, Patricia Arrington, Julie Silk, Matthew Martens, Suzanne MacLeod, Carol Finklestein and Charlotte Jorden.

Also, thanks to Kathy Sachs who helped me with the computer. (Boy, why did they ever invent them?)

To my brother Don who helped me by making copies of the book and suggesting general things along the way and to my brother Art who set up Microsoft word for me.

To Jennifer Leigh Mustoe who edited the book and never was hesitant in her constructive criticism and encouragement.

Last but not least it behooves me to mention John Walter, a lifelong pal from "the good old days" and the role model for Eddie Howard in TWENTY HILLCREST ROAD.

Twenty Hillcrest Road

CHAPTER ONE

I suppose by all measured standards that many years ago I was just an average kid growing up in the small town of Danvers in the 40s and 50s. Perhaps I never approved of anyone's ever labeling me as such but there was really nothing I could've done to counter such a description. To believe I was above others in certain abilities was only the natural way for me to go; nonetheless, one unwritten rule I should've followed—but didn't—was to never make stark comparisons or to strive unrealistically toward a goal which I instinctively knew I wouldn't reach—ever. So it was with me. In most respects I was no different than those around me: we all had our yearnings and feelings. Simply, that's the way it was.

However, then there were the unmeasured things that sometimes crept up, leaving me confused and unable to adapt. They came in varied forms: certain people opposed me in ways that hurt; circumstances arose over which I had little or no control; and an accident occurred that totally changed my agenda. I'll relate how they cropped up in my childhood and continued throughout the ensuing years.

The truth should be known: I'm giving this account for both entertaining and instructive purposes.

For in the end does it really matter what anyone thinks, anyway?

It was a hot, humid day in late July and 1950 was only five months distant. The year I was ten years old was a time when the kids in the neighborhood were free to do just about anything, or nothing at all. That meant we spent most of our time in the summer playing baseball. It didn't seem to take much to make us happy back then.

Being the middle of three sons was sometimes agonizing. Since I was sensitive like my mother, I learned only through a painful process how to deal with the good as well as with the bad. Mine were the challenges of any average kid. And yet it took me almost a lifetime to come to terms with some of them.

Mom, as did the women of that era, performed the cooking and cleaning chores. She was a person who had her sons' and their father's interests always on her mind. She wanted us to be content. That fact alone meant some suffering on her part.

We lived in a small, cream-colored house overlooking a scenic hill on Hillcrest Road in East Danvers. Across the street diagonally on Cardinal Road stood the Annese place, a large brown structure that featured a beautiful lawn and a garage in back. Mr. Annese was a quiet, hard-working Italian gentleman who, with his attractive wife, had three children. Nancy and Sam took after their gentle father; Kenny, my best friend, was boisterous like me. I never did know what

Mr. Annese did for a living, though it didn't really matter. I was certain he was a decent man. In those days we never thought that adults had first names. They were Mr. and Mrs. to all us kids. They existed in another world, separated from us by a wisdom we didn't possess. We looked up to them. No kid would've ever had the audacity to show disrespect toward any elder.

During summer vacation my mother oftentimes went out of her way to please her boys, especially when it came to our meals.

Around six-thirty in the morning I heard Mom moving about in the kitchen. I was hoping that meant my two brothers and I were going to have French toast, my favorite breakfast. There also was the wonderful scent of bacon frying in the saucepan. Soon Scott, twelve, and Andy, seven, would be joining me at the table, where there were three large glasses of orange juice and a bottle of Log Cabin maple syrup staring at us from the middle of the table. Dad didn't always eat with the family, something I could never understand. "Is Dad coming to the table this morning?" I asked, looking at my mother. She turned slowly toward me and shook her head no, which caused a sinking feeling in my gut. That often happened and it sometimes angered me. I never asked Scott or Andy if it bothered them, though it probably didn't. At any rate, I figured Dad was either upstairs doing something or had already left for work at his welding company in nearby Salem.

The field, the spot where our team competed for hours

each day, was a hop-skip-and-jump across from where we lived. All the houses in the neighborhood were fairly close together. Everyone lived on or near Hillcrest Road, Cardinal Road, and Elliott Street. It only took a matter of minutes for all of us to reach the field.

That morning we knew by the rising temperature it was going to be another muggy day. As usual, Scott was the controlling factor, the member of the team who dictated how long we participated and who played what position. There was no question that he was the boss, the big shot. Being one of his younger brothers, I always scoffed at that assumption. It didn't bother the other guys as much, except maybe Tommy "Blubberguts" Amero. I actually thought he sometimes hated Scott.

Scott required all the boys of the East Danvers Red Sox to assemble on the grass field as close to eight as possible, but his idea of the perfect practice was always ruined by the fact that it never happened. Some players arrived late. Scott waited impatiently as each kid ascended the hill.

Every morning, Scott stood by the home plate area of our field (we didn't really have bases), with his Dom Dimaggio wooden bat in his hand. As each boy approached him, he pointed the bat out as if it were his scepter and he were the king.

"Gee, Scott, do we have to play so early?" Blubberguts, the biggest guy on the team, blurted out.

"Blubberguts!" he barked. "Take center field!"

Blubberguts trotted to his designated position, moving his large body in the shimmering sun as if it hurt.

"Little Billy" Grant arrived and Scott yelled out, "What took you so long? You stay put. I haven't decided where I want you." Little Billy stood there and simply nodded.

"Big Billy" Grant crouched slightly under Scott's wrath. "Where you want me to play, Scott?" he inquired.

Scott suddenly turned and waved his arms toward Blubberguts who was standing in center field and shouted, "Never mind, get back in here and we'll choose up sides."

Blubberguts jogged back toward home plate and limped over to Scott like a sick dog.

By the time everyone arrived, Scott had yelled at each player. "We have too many sissies here," he affirmed. "It's got to stop or else!" I wondered why we tolerated his verbal lashings, but he was the boss and we all respected the boss.

Leaning on the bat as if it were a gentleman's cane, Scott pulled off his cap and his bushy brown hair shone in the sun. Pulling his lean arm over his face, he wiped his brow with his shirtsleeve and pulled the cap back on one-handed.

It amazed me that even though we possessed the freedom to play the game of baseball each and every day, the mere thought that we weren't under the authority of any adults, Scott's presence still tempered our independence. It was irritating. How could one guy be so powerful? It simply wasn't fair.

"Okay, guys, let's get going. Everyone here?" Scott looked around and seemed pleased. "Good. Today I want

Blubberguts and Ben to pick the players they want. Got it?" Blubberguts and I stepped forward and approached Scott.

By nine the sun was beginning to show its strength. It was the first day of August. All ten of us were present. Besides my two brothers and myself, "the Robblee boys," there were Tommy Amero, "Big Billy" Grant and his little brother, Bobby, their cousin, "Little Billy" Grant, Danny Doheney, Kenny Annese, my buddy, and Joey Buccella. A confident group of youths blended into a workable unit. Everyone was different, but together we were a great team.

If we were lucky, Ernie Izzo and Nicky Venti, both in their late teens and inseparable friends, attended our practices and demonstrated their superior skills. We all admired them. To us pipsqueaks, they were young men who could teach us the proper techniques of hitting and fielding. They kidded with us, made us feel comfortable. They lived next door to each other off Elliott Street. We tabbed them the "coaches" of the East Danvers Red Sox. Even if only one of them showed up on any given day, we felt secure because we knew we'd learn something that day. Neither Ernie nor Nicky criticized our playing ability in such a way that it embarrassed us. They gave us sound advice on everything to do with baseball. I always had difficulty with lifting my head whenever a hard ground ball came my way. Ernie tried his best to instruct me how not to be afraid of the ball. If I jerked my head upward, he warned me, it definitely could be disastrous. The ball could take a crazy bounce off the uneven surface and whack me right in the noggin. This was an ongoing problem with me, a fear that I somehow managed with great difficulty to overcome throughout my shortened baseball career in junior high and high school, including my two years with Ferncroft in the Danvers Twilight League.

All of us marveled at how Nicky stroked the ball. Ernie delivered a pitch. Smack. Nicky drove it a mile, even further than Scott ever did. We all stood there, motionless, in different positions on the field. We stared as the baseball soared deep toward left field, way beyond the tall grass. Funny, but I believed all of us kids had the same feeling. I gloated inside. It was then I realized that Nicky was the only guy who was able to outdo Scott and out-boss him. I was positive that Scott was well aware of that fact. But he never said anything to any of us about Nicky's performance.

If enough players didn't show up (there were anywhere between six and ten members between the ages of seven and twelve) we took batting practice or had contests to see which one could hit the longest ball. Only Scott was capable of hitting a home run, of which we all were bitterly aware. A ball was judged out of the park when it reached the tall grass in the outfield, far away. How many feet that was, we didn't know nor did we care. Blubberguts once almost made a home run. After Scott repeatedly accomplished that seemingly impossible feat, he cupped his hands to his mouth and yelled the exact number of the round-tripper he'd just smashed. It was sickening. "That's fourteen," he smirked as he slowly circled the bases.

I started our game by tossing one of our taped, old wooden bats (two of our six bats were taped at the top) to

Blubberguts, who caught it in mid-air with one hand. The one with the last fist to cover the top of the bat without any overlapping chose first. However, there was one stipulation we followed before we began choosing sides. Scott and Danny always had to be on opposite teams. Both southpaws, they could throw the ball with authority.

"I choose Kenny," I said aloud. I pointed to my friend and the diminutive, rugged fellow with the buttons on his baseball shirt unbuttoned to his stomach joined me at home plate. He had a wide smile on his face. Patting me on the shoulder, Kenny said, "Thanks, buddy."

Blubberguts stood there beside me and began to scratch his chin. Besides Scott he was classified as the other slugger. After hesitating a few more moments, he countered with, " I take Scott." He peered at his choice and motioned weakly for Scott to stand next to him.

Besides Kenny, I chose Danny Doheney, Big Billy Grant and his little brother, Bobby. Blubberguts completed his team by picking Joey Buccella, Little Billy Grant, and my little brother, Andy. Sad to say, Andy was always the last to be chosen, being the smallest and least experienced kid of the lot. But he was a spirited bugger who in his unpredictability was capable of coming up with the crucial base hit in the game. He was a natural who in a few years would become the star of the Little League Athletics, the same club I played for four years earlier.

By all accounts, I believed the Blubberguts team had a slight advantage over mine. Clearly, they had the better hitters and the superior players. Notwithstanding the fact that the team Scott was on always won, the trio of my older brother and Joey and Blubberguts appeared to be too potent for us to defeat. Scott's overall ability and arrogance were unbeatable and we all knew it. But I forever had a smidgen of hope that someday that would change. In everyone's mind the boss prevailed. It was as if the opposing team subconsciously caved in and lost. To add further insult Scott always refused to leave the field until he had been declared the winner. I was the brother of a big-time winner and sore loser.

We got down to the daily ritual of playing the game of baseball. As far as I was concerned, it was a grinding process. Hitting and fielding and pitching and waiting in the hot sun. "I'm sick of this," Kenny would say to me. "I'd rather just go to Folly Hill." I always nodded but kept it between the two of us. I wondered how the other guys really felt about showing up every stinking day. Did it matter? I didn't think any of us realized at the time what the future would bring. We were at that stage in our lives when nothing but the present mattered. We simply believed we belonged there. Nobody worried about where he'd be in five or ten years. Maybe, just maybe, this unending activity on the field of competition would lead to an unexpected reward down the road. We had dreams. A few of us had the blown-up notion of becoming another Ted Williams, Mel Parnell, or Bobby Doerr. Did we actually believe this was possible? Absolutely. Amazingly, several of the East Danvers Red Sox graduated to the Little League, then to the Pony League, and, finally, to the Danvers Twilight League. That was the big time! Some of us later on would become fierce opponents. Kenny who later on became a member of the Little League Champion Browns and I were eventually placed on different teams. As a member of the second-place Athletics, I resented losing to my best friend's team.

Clearly, baseball defined us. What else was there? We felt superior. Perhaps having to report to the field on a daily basis and physically participating against other players was a positive thing. Without knowing it we were developing a sense of confidence in a competitive way.

By mid-morning, the sun was stifling, making everyone sweat. Every so often, when there was a break in the action, I dashed across Hillcrest Road to grab some lemonade. That sudden move of mine inevitably caused insults from some of the guys.

"Hey, Ben, what are you, special or something?" Blubberguts cracked.

"There goes the baby to get a drink," Joey yelled.

"Get some for me," Big Billy quipped.

The teasing never stopped, which made me feel funny and a bit guilty inside. It didn't take me long to scamper across the street, gulp down a glass of the yellow stuff, and rush back (within a few minutes of my return the barbs ceased).

But for some inexplicable reason we kids didn't mind the heat. Later on in life I took for granted it was one of the advantages of being young. We thought of ourselves as indestructible, a gift that adults unwittingly relinquished as they got older.

My mother was seated at the kitchen table. She always minded the heat to the extent that it rendered her immobile. Mom appeared exhausted from the humidity, so much so that she actually despised the summer. Her light brown hair, usually shiny and flowing, was all messed up from the moisture in the air. In those days nobody in the neighborhood had air conditioners. We Robblees had three or four fans strategically placed throughout the house to counter the heat. People suffered and that was that.

There were two infielders, two outfielders, and a pitcher. That comprised a total team. The tall, worn screen behind home plate, a side of a cardboard box or any appropriate article we could find, served as the catcher. The three bases were small stones that were marked by white chalk. In the case of any ordinary call, we were our own umpires. It went without saying that Scott was the final arbiter whenever a crucial decision was necessary. And we all were resigned to what that would be. If it favored his team, so be it. His strong voice overpowered all of us. We mumbled to ourselves over the injustice of our situation, but not where he could hear us.

Kenny was stationed at shortstop for my selected team. I was at second base. Danny Doheney, a tall, skinny kid who constantly was biting his fingernails until they bled, loomed ahead of us as the menacing pitcher, always ready to strike out the opposing batter. Because there were only five players on each side, we were spread out in the field. So Kenny was really playing shortstop and third base. I was covering second and first base. We had to go with what we had. If an opposing batter were to drill a grounder toward Kenny, I'd have to rush over to first in order to make the putout.

After each pitched ball, a designated kid, usually either Andy or Bobby Grant, the youngest players from the team at bat, retrieved the ball near the screen and threw it back to the pitcher. That job was difficult all by itself. Scott, Blubberguts, and Danny never stooped that low, never even thought of going after the ball. They were up in the hierarchy, among the elite, "the immortals." I, along with Kenny and Little Billy Grant, would sometimes chase down the ball just to be accommodating, so that nothing hostile came of it. Maybe it was a question of who was strong and who was weak. There were certain inequities that we had to accept. Perhaps I wasn't asserting my rights, though I wasn't aware of that at the time.

The field, our sacred ground, slanted both dramatically upward from the infield to the outfield and downward from home plate to right field. A straight line of dry dirt ran from home plate all the way to second base. There was no pitcher's mound. The rest of the field consisted of a healthy assortment of tall and short grass with an annoying array of weeds. Trees everywhere stood as sentinels in deep left field and centerfield. The grass was very deep in certain spots. To add a little humor to each game, whenever someone hit the ball for a base hit, he had to scamper down hill to first, round that base, and then run up hill to second. It didn't seem funny to us at the time, but, in retrospect, it was hysterical.

As noontime approached, it became hotter and more humid, which meant we became sweatier and grubbier. That was an indication that we were having fun.

We all lived within a short walking distance from the field. To us Robblees it was as if we were playing each day at our own ballpark. We lived directly across the street at the very top of a hill. From our viewing point, we could gaze upon the houses below. If one of my parents were to snap a picture from our living room window or from our front lawn, a panorama as represented in a postcard would be produced.

Our session of playing ball wasn't over. Because there were maybe ten or fifteen minutes to go, there always arose a feeling of anticipation and fear as lunchtime neared. It didn't center on the idea that our mothers had forgotten to make us our lunches. All the guys on the two teams clearly knew that a quick meal of a nutritious sandwich, a cold drink, and a dessert would be awaiting them in their respective homes. No, that wasn't the concern that mounted as the hour came closer. It was Scott. Would he permit us to leave on time? Just as General George S. Patton was a supreme field commander, my older brother had the same power over each of us. The East Danvers Red Sox, an excellent team made up of varying degrees of baseball talent, were under the single thumb of Mr. Scott E. Robblee, Jr.

"Joey, Joey." A distinct, loud sound, familiar to each of us, was heard coming from a considerable distance. It was the unmistakable warning emanating from the mouth of Mrs. Buccella. "Joey!"

It was a ritual that had become part of our daily existence. It didn't shock us nor did it affect our play. At first it didn't even concern us. Nothing came to a screeching halt. Something repeated many times over soon loses its initial importance. So it was with the screeching of Mrs. Buccella.

The mother was demanding that her son come "straight home this instant." She wasn't visible but her bellowing was sufficient in sending a clear message. Blubberguts suddenly started to laugh out loud. Soon most of us joined in. This put a tremendous amount of pressure on poor Joey. A tall-for-his-age kid, he was sometimes so emotional that he was capable of losing his temper for no apparent reason. We all knew that he was straining inside, attempting to withhold any outburst in front of his peers. We also realized that it was only a matter of a few minutes before he'd explode.

"Joey."

It was getting serious. We fellows, frozen and spread out over the entire field, looked at Scott, then at Joey. The zero hour was nearing, the confrontational time when the butting heads of my older brother and Mrs. Buccella would come face-to-face.

Moments passed. Nothing.

"Scott, I have to go." Joey looked up Hillcrest Road as

if he were expecting his mother to appear momentarily. He appeared beside himself.

"Not yet," Scott said, picking up a bat.

"Come on, Scott."

To us kids, this was becoming a crisis. Soon Scott would have to tell us what to do. We waited impatiently. I couldn't speak for the others, but I was hoping Mrs. Buccella was going to give Scott the business.

"One more at bat for me," Scott said. "It won't take long for me to hit another homer. Then you all can go home." Scott made several practice swings and slowly strode to the plate. He stared at Danny and said, "Let's go."

Danny readied himself to pitch. The stylish lefty with the big front teeth was as determined to strike out Scott as Scott was to murder the ball. Everyone knew it was going to be a steamer. They were the two superior athletes on the team, although Joey, our regular catcher in games, thought he was the best player. To be honest, most of the East Danvers Red Sox were fierce competitors, some excelling in more than one sport when they attended Holten-Richmond Junior High School and Holten High School.

The hour of noon suggested that we all were hungry. Danny stood on the flat dirt, glaring at the opposing batter. He hesitated at first, then lifted his right leg high, pumped, but decided not to let it fly.

"Scott, my mom's going to kill me if I'm late."

Scott grinned, didn't say anything, and crouched at the plate. He was ready. I, along with Kenny, Bobby and Big Billy

Grant, waited behind Danny for something to happen.

Scott waved his bat furiously as Danny finally delivered a strike right down the pike. Smash. The bat met the ball. Scott prevailed once again. It was a high liner to deep centerfield where Bobby Grant was standing. The little fellow looked toward the sky. He struggled to get a glimpse of the ball. The sun made it impossible for him to see. Where was it? After only a few seconds, we had the answer. The ball descended.

Thud. It hit Bobby directly against the middle of his forehead, then ricocheted high into the air and, ultimately, landed in the deep grass in home run territory. It was another super clout for Scott.

It happened so fast that Scott completed his circling of the bases without ever noticing what had transpired.

"Number fifteen," he yelled, upon reaching home plate.

The inter-squad game was over because Scott said so. When he, at long last, saw Bobby sitting stunned in the out-field he rushed to the rescue. Quickly he checked out the status of Bobby's aching head. Bobby was crying but seemed to be all right. If a doctor had been present to examine him, he would've found a small red bump. No, it was a big bump. Scott quickly gave it a look. Seemed okay to him. He rubbed Bobby's forehead, nodded approvingly, and then ordered us to go home for lunch.

CHAPTER TWO

When I was a boy there was one annual event that stood out in my mind.

Mom, as was our family's custom before the school year began, always brought me and Scott and Andy to Conrad's, a clothing store for boys and girls in the next town over, Beverly. All three of us were overjoyed because we knew in the approaching fall we'd be wearing new clothes. Upon entering Conrad's I was awed by the mere amount of clothes and became excited over the many choices and colors that faced the customer. There were countless articles of apparel for the kids: pants, shirts, sweaters, shoes, coats, hats, dresses, underwear, etc. All the kids I ever saw there went bonkers and never complained about the amount of time they spent shopping with their parents. I never saw any tears ever being shed.

On that particular day the four of us (Dad never came along) covered the two floors of the store in about two hours. The one item that I loved the most was a pair of red-and-brown plaid pants (in those days no student ever attended school dressed in dungarees or sneakers). Neatness and cleanliness seemed prevalent.

One afternoon during the first month of school I came home from Williams School. I was wearing those plaid pants. It had been a typical day of fun and studying different subjects. I was surprised to see my father waiting for me in the living room. Seldom was he at home in the afternoon. Without any explanation he said, "Ben, I want you to go down cellar and sweep the floor. It's too dirty down there."

"Now?" I asked.

"Now," he demanded. "I'm sick of all the mess."

"Okay, but first Dad I have to go to my room to change these clothes."

"No, Ben, I want you to do it right away." He stared at me and pointed in the direction of the cellar door.

I hastened down the cellar and completed the chore. I was devastated! The pants were filthy and appeared ruined. I was so angry that I further smudged the pants by rubbing more dirt on them. I cried all afternoon and was sullen at suppertime. Even though the plaid pants were eventually cleaned, I refused to wear them very much after that.

Our father, Scott Robblee, Sr., was responsible for the formation of the East Danvers Red Sox in the first place. It was his generous nature to be good to kids and it gave him immense satisfaction to see the local boys participating in something for which he was responsible. He'd been an only child who had struggled mightily through his lonely childhood. I didn't know this, of course, until much later on in my life. Dad took considerable time off from the operation of his welding business in Salem to help organize and encourage everyone to play ball. Several times he related to his three sons how he'd never had the opportunity to play in such an environment. I doubted whether my brothers ever understood this, but I interpreted his past as a time that hadn't been very delightful. Not much fun and laughter had existed in his household. His father, a blacksmith, had been very stern, even cold toward his son. Hard work, discipline, and solemnity had controlled Dad's small universe.

Never did I forget a particular story Dad confessed to me on one gloomy evening in late summer. It was not his practice to divulge anything too personal to anyone, including, I always thought, even Mom. He spoke in generalities and kept his emotions to himself.

It was raining and the air inside the house was unbelievably stifling. We were seated in the living room, just the two of us. He was a robust man who was over six feet tall and weighed well over two hundred pounds. He often wore short sleeve shirts that displayed his muscular arms and old chino pants while relaxing around the house. He had extremely thick brown hair with a dramatic V at the top of his forehead. The one superior thing about Dad, though, was his physical strength. Oftentimes, some of the kids, especially Blubberguts, tested their strength by having a handshaking contest with him to see who was able to squeeze the hardest. Dad squished every hand that ever came into contact with his right hand. He seemed to revel in this ability to outdo anyone willing to take him on.

Whenever I was with him, alone, I felt both safe and uneasy. It was a strange sensation, to say the least. There was some fear involved, because I was worried about one thing. What if by chance I uttered a comment out of the blue that would lead into a punishable offense? His reaction could be gentle or gruff. I never knew which one it would be. There was a presence about him that was threatening. But, conversely, he was always there to protect me, or so I believed. This strange duality was a huge miscalculation on my part. But then, I was ten.

That evening was wet and foreboding. It was as if the thunderstorm outside encapsulated the two of us in our own little world. No one would be able to enter our realm.

After several moments of noticeable silence Dad said, "This rain reminds me of the frog."

"Frog? What frog?" I inquired.

He related, in bursts of broken speech, how, as a nine-year-old kid growing up in South Salem, he had suddenly come upon a frog while walking along the marshland close to his house. His father, the grandpa I never knew, had always warned him to stay clear of that area.

The rain was beating against the window. Staring straight ahead my father said, "I was walking along in the marsh, even though my father forbade me to go there. I was head-strong, stubborn if you want to know the truth, Ben." He snickered. "I went there anyway. Nobody was going to tell me what to do." Dad jabbed at his chest with his thumb in a way that made my skin crawl slightly.

"It was soggy out there, but I liked being by myself. I felt strong, like a hero. I was getting away with something. But," my father said, hesitating. "But, after it happened, only then did it dawn on me what I'd done. How dumb I'd been. My father had been right all along."

"What happened, Dad?" I was sitting there on the floor looking up at him.

"As I was walking along, the ground was getting wet. I was soaked. Straight ahead, I detected a large green-and -brown frog hopping around. As I kept my eyes on it, I became more fascinated. It was so free, able to jump about."

"What happened, Dad?"

My father remained silent.

"What happened out there… on the marsh?" I said impatiently.

"Well," my father continued, itching his chest, "I followed the frog. It was jumping all over the place. I don't know why, even to this day, Ben, why I did what I did. It was absolutely wrong." He looked down at me as if he were imploring me to trust him with what he was about to tell me.

Getting up quickly and going over to him and touching his arm, I said, "Please tell me, Dad, what you did."

Using a handkerchief that he had retrieved from his pants' pocket, my father wiped his forehead. "After several minutes, I grabbed the frog and squeezed as hard as I could.

I kept squeezing and squeezing. Until it was dead."

I stood there, not knowing how to respond. I felt badly for him. What could I do? I certainly didn't dare berate him. So my reaction was not to react. I pulled my hand away from my father's arm, hoping he didn't notice.

"I still don't know why I did it. I just did, that's all." As he looked at me, he kept wiping his forehead. It must've been ninety degrees in the room. "The thing is, it kept looking at me when I first held it in my hands. It was squirming about every which way, trying to escape. I could feel its panic. The poor thing was terrified."

I said nothing, but I started to feel sick. I put myself in the frog's place as if I could feel my father's powerful hands actually squeezing the crap out of me. At that very moment I was petrified.

"That's it," my father said. "After the frog was dead, I held it for a long, long time. I couldn't let it go. I felt terrible. I cried out loud for what seemed forever. I was afraid to go home to my father."

The rain outside kept pelting against the window. Never had I anticipated such an admission from my father. I didn't have the slightest clue as to what to say or do. Although it didn't occur to me at the time, the man before me, the person responsible for my very existence, had carried a tremendous load of intense guilt within him throughout a lifetime over a helpless frog. I learned an important lesson from that episode. I discovered, shockingly, that my father wasn't infallible.

My father paid for most of the uniforms of the East Danvers Red Sox. Of the ten participants on the team, four wore white outfits with a "Red Sox" logo on their shirt. The remaining six wore gray duds without such a designation. Nobody had baseball cleats. In fact, I never recalled anyone's ever wearing them in those bygone days. No such things as colorful socks existed; bare legs were the norm. It was the era of black and white. Technicolor was unknown. Frills were unheard of. You played the national pastime with what you had. Plain stuff satisfied everyone.

Even though, individually, we presented to every opponent a group who differed in appearance, as a unit the team's chemistry came together. Everyone was in harmonious step. We weren't flashy. That image automatically camouflaged our competence in the field. We didn't appear to be a worthy adversary. But we were. Bigger and better teams always misjudged our overall attitude, our ability. But, unmistakably, once the game got underway, reality set in. We felt confident of victory.

Some of us had flat white sneakers. Others had to settle for their everyday shoes. Everyone wore Red Sox caps except Little Billy and Kenny, who went bareheaded. How their heads didn't burn from the sun was beyond me. Blubberguts' belly drooped over his pants. What a slob! Little Billy wore brown shoes and soiled white socks and had the puniest legs in East Danvers. He looked like an Al Capp cartoon character. He also had the distinct ability to wear his wool Red Sox shirt in the summer heat without an undershirt on.

Just the thought of that gave me goose bumps. Big Billy was the sneak of the East Danvers Red Sox. I never trusted a word he uttered. A couple of times he was caught stealing a couple of pieces of candy from Ellison's Grocery, so Mr. Ellison didn't allow him to come into the store for a month or so. After that, Mr. Ellison watched every movement he ever made. Not much could be said about Bobby Grant, who had a perpetual sleepy look about him and followed his older brother Billy around as if he were stuck to him. Danny Doheney, a tall, skinny kid and an only child, was one of the dominant members of the team. His father, a small, frail man, worked in a box factory in Danvers and his mother, a large woman who controlled her son's every action, was a nurse who was depended upon to protect Danny in the event of any mishap. In an argument it was rumored that Mrs. Doheney was capable of pummeling her husband into submission. I was convinced that Danny got his independent nature from her. Scott somehow never came down hard on him, something I not only questioned but also envied. Danny was quiet until something came up that challenged his ability as a baseball player. "I'm just as good a pitcher as Scott is," he confided to me. Did he ever impart that opinion to my older brother?

We ignored the remaining youngsters in our neighborhood. What were they doing all this time? We never knew the chubby, quiet Bauer boy over in the yellow house across the street from our house. He came and went with his two older sisters and parents without a word. Never even a glance from them. The Bauer kids were never outside during the day. They had to be doing something to keep busy. It was a mystery to all of us. Collectively we team members thought they were very weird.

What about the Vitelli family who lived in the green-and-brown house located in the barren field hundreds of yards away in the distance? Mounds of dirt and dust blew about everywhere. How many were in their brood? Was it four or five boys? Short little guys, they were. All we knew was that their father, a rugged man, owned a construction company. It was a very successful business, too, because all day long the ugly green Vitelli trucks, full of gravel, came roaring up Cardinal Road and passed by our baseball field. We heard them as they started their climb up the steep hill all the way from Elliott Street. We gazed in wonderment at the men sitting in front and the boys standing in back. A scary, tough group, one I'd certainly never want to mess with. They represented an alien world, separate from our universe, strangers to be secretly scorned.

CHAPTER THREE

We spent our afternoons doing different things. The mornings were strictly for baseball. After lunch some of the kids returned to the ball field to practice even more. The rest stayed at home, or went their separate ways. Bumming around, we called it.

Kenny and I always had plenty of ground to cover: roaming the immediate area near our homes was a wonderful way of having fun. We sometimes imagined we were two explorers. One afternoon after baseball and lunch we walked slowly up Hillcrest Road, adjacent to the field. About fifty yards up that dirt road, after passing a small cornfield and three nondescript houses on our left, we came to a half-finished brick building on the right. To the right side of that ugly structure, if, instead of our going straight ahead on Hillcrest Road in the direction of Joey Buccella's house, we decided to turn and step over the rough surface of rocks and gravel for twenty or so paces, we stumbled upon a severe decline called Lupine Road. It was a partial roadway that could only be entered by way of Elliott Street, the main thruway. "Hilldale" would've been a perfect name for that section of Danvers. In the extreme corner of Lupine

Road lived the Warner family, whose large green-and-white house, with tall hedges flawlessly manicured and beautiful flowers of many colors surrounding a brilliant lawn, clearly surpassed all the other homes in East Danvers—not to mention that the two Warner daughters, Wanda and Elaine, lived there. I was in awe of Wanda, who was Scott's age.

Unbelievably we never visited each other's homes. Except to go into Kenny's cellar, by way of a rear door, to play Ping-Pong (I wasn't able to beat him), I never entered his house. I didn't have a clue as to what his living room or kitchen or bedroom looked like. During those carefree days, we had a respect, considered other families' residences as being private, off limits, not to be invaded even by friends. The two Grant families, brothers Big Billy and Bobby, and cousin Little Billy, lived the farthest away on Congress Avenue, an area I wasn't familiar with. Blubberguts, known for his drinking bouts of soda pop, resided above his father's variety store on Elliott Street.

And the strangest thing sometimes occurred outside the Buccella house, way in back, during the early afternoon hours.

Though Kenny and I often passed by Danny's house on Elliott Street en route to Ellison's Grocery, never did we consider stopping by to see him unless we'd been invited. Maybe that was why nobody needed to lock any doors or worry about personal safety. It seemed like an ideal community;

how fortunate we were to have grown up there.

The situation with the chickens was one of the most fascinating events in my young life. One afternoon right after lunch, Kenny and I walked slowly up Hillcrest Road, stopped, shaded our eyes from the blinding sun with our hands to study the two men working in the heat on the brick house to our right, then raced down the hill leading to Joey's house. Promptly we hid behind a small brown shed, about thirty yards from the anticipated scene. Our hearts were pounding. That was a sure sign it would be a short time before Mrs. DeVito, Joey Buccella's grandmother, showed up. We felt like spies on a dangerous mission.

The old woman didn't disappoint us. We only waited for ten minutes or so when she appeared out of the cellar bulkhead. Wearing an old wrinkled dress over her large, flabby body, she dragged her feet along in an ancient pair of red slippers. Her puffy bare legs revealed the largest veins, a deep purple, we'd ever seen.

"She has to be at least eighty years old," Kenny whispered to me.

I tried not to laugh. We peered at this mysterious woman who came from another country. She was about to do something ghastly. We thought she was crazy. She was jabbering in Italian, which made it more intriguing—plus her mission seemed to be purely instinctive.

The yard at the back of the house was fenced in. Beyond it, for what seemed to extend for miles, was a wide-open field. The Buccella family certainly enjoyed privacy. It was as if that particular location, hidden at such a low level, was placed there by some secret power to give the impression of being in its own little world.

There were chickens parading about right next to Mrs. DeVito. Perhaps a dozen of them were prancing about like lunatics. Back and forth they went, their heads bobbing in unison. Kenny began to giggle, which caused me to do the same.

"Shut-up," I said, putting my index finger to my lips in an attempt to get my friend to hush up. What if we were caught? The old woman certainly would tattle on us, bringing forth the wrath of Mrs. Buccella and we'd be unable to see what was going to happen next.

She looked up suddenly. Did she hear us? We forced ourselves to become motionless. The chickens continued to cluck and squawk as if they knew what they were about to face.

Mrs. DeVito, a powerhouse of a woman, slowly slipped across the grass and snatched up one of the unsuspecting chickens. That task was easy for her. She probably could've taken on a much worthier opponent. Using her hands and the strength of her fat arms, she succeeded in snapping the skinny neck of the poor creature until its head just swung about by its skin. Where just moments before it had fluttered about with its contented mates, the chicken was now lifeless. Kenny and I merely stared at each other. It was a shocking scene! We didn't understand how anyone had the ability to do that, commit such an act of cruelty. I kept feeling my throat to make sure it was still there. Was I next? Kenny stood silently as his eyes remained targeted on the old woman. She then attached a wooden fastener to the chicken's neck, walked over to the clothesline by the basement and finished by hanging the fowl upside down on the line. That was it. Then she went back to get another chicken.

Within a short space of time, all of the chickens had met their fate: they were dead. They were hanging on the line in a perfect row, their mouths dripping a disgusting fluid. It wasn't until my teen-age years that I was able to shrug off the ritual that Kenny and I had seen enacted on a bi-weekly basis. The first time I'd become sick to my stomach. As for Kenny, I wasn't sure how he really felt. But with each repetition the shock value diminished. I no longer was apprehensive about it. Within several months it became apparent that I was looking forward to the next time. I felt guilty over my apparent delight in witnessing such a thing. I asked myself many times: since when did someone become fascinated over a killing? Kenny and I never discussed the subject between us, so I always wondered if Kenny possessed the same doubts that I had. We never spoke of it after the fact because it would've exposed an emotional weakness.

CHAPTER FOUR

I was sitting at my small desk in my room, where I spent a lot of time when not involved outside playing baseball or doing something else with Kenny. It was my refuge. Like most kids of the 40s and 50s I invented my own form of entertainment. I wasn't any different than anyone else when it came to the necessity of keeping busy, of having fun. I was different in that my strong suit was my ability to enter into my own exciting world of dice baseball. In fact, I never thought that competition was a true measuring stick of one's worth. When I held those two dice in my hands and threw them on the desk to see what numbers appeared, it was a magical process. My whole body pulsated with joy and my voice oftentimes screeched as I described each moment of each game. I was in my glory because no one was present to interrupt me. I always kept a record of everything as if it were my own personal treasure.

My game between the Boston Red Sox and hated New York Yankees began. The two lineups were in front of me on ruled paper.

"The attendance today is around thirty four thousand, a sellout," I began, looking around the room as if it were

Fenway Park. "All around the stands, from first base to right field, from third base to left field and straight ahead in deep center by the flagpole, the fans are cheering. What a sight! Yankee blue flags waving against bright red banners. The weather for this early August afternoon is cloudy with a slight chance of rain. The wind is mighty intense and is blowing in from center field toward home plate." I threw the dice and they landed on the desk. It was a six and a one. "The first batter, Gil MacDougald, the Yankee third baseman, hits a sharp grounder to Vern Stephens at shortstop and Stephens drills it to big Walt Dropo at first. One out. Mel Parnell, the southpaw hurler, wipes his brow. He picks up the rosin bag on the mound and readies himself to face Bobby Brown."

The game proceeded through nine innings with unabated excitement. Two sixes with the dice represented a home run. One combination was a strikeout, another a fly out, still another a groundout and so on. A single, a double, and a triple also came up. There were all sorts of possibilities. With each thrown ball to each batter I wrote down the result. I never wanted the contest to end.

I raised my voice. "Here comes Hank Bauer, the left fielder for the Bronx Bombers to the plate. Well, folks, the game is tied four to four and it's the top of the ninth. It's now or never for both teams. The sky is threatening rain and is getting very dark. Will this mean a delay in the game if there's a downpour? Let's hope not, fans. Denny Galehouse, the right-handed flame thrower in for Mel Parnell in relief, stares at Bauer. The square-jawed ex-marine stares back. A sudden silence comes over the park. I mean, folks, this is drama at its finest. Galehouse delivers a steamer toward the meat of the plate. Wham. Hank connects and sends a towering blast over the Green Monster and into the screen in left field." The crowd in my mind booed at his success. "Bauer circles the bases, his right arm raised in triumph. The whole place is in pandemonium." I explained this moment with such intensity that I began to lose my breath. Also, I peered around the room, afraid that Scott or Andy or Mom might be close by to hear me. I didn't want to be embarrassed by my actions, not to mention the fact that I needed to be alone at a crucial part of the game.

The Yankees defeated the Sox, 5-4. I didn't allow the outcome to affect me adversely; I had to be as objective as possible.

I kept batting averages of every player on my four American League teams. The Red Sox, my favorite team, the St. Louis Browns, the Yankees, and the Chicago White Sox rounded out my own private league. I felt as if I were the sole human being in the universe playing such a game that day. Who else could've thought up such a clever tool of enjoyment? It was a proud moment in my life, and, without doubt, one of the happiest.

A batting champion was declared officially at the end of the season and a home-run leader and a strikeout king. I was methodical in arranging all the statistics on paper in pencil and always remembered with fondness that Ned Garver of the St. Louis Browns was the top hurler in the league and Sherm Lollar, a catcher for the Chicago White Sox, won the batting title. And the biggest kick I got out of all this was that I was the official announcer of every contest. I was in complete control of my domain.

I was thrilled whenever the game went into extra innings or was decided by a hit in the last of the ninth inning. Each game produced its own drama. I was a major part of the action. I was there! If the truth were to be revealed, I would readily admit that I loved dice baseball much more than actually playing with the guys. But I never told this to a soul—if I had, letting anyone in on my secret would've ruined everything.

One of our exciting events included "sour pickle time." By mid-afternoon, if there were nothing else on the docket, Kenny and I met outside his house. We walked down Cardinal Road, which was a picturesque hill shaded by tall, lovely trees. We never stopped talking. If the sky were overcast on any given day, the stroll toward Elliott Street gave us the impression of its being completely dark. Or, we imagined the same, like we'd taken off at night against our parents' wishes. No kid ever left his household after eight at night in pursuit of any adventure. We figured we'd get into trouble, but how much trouble we never knew. We never tested to find out.

Sometimes, to add variety to our jaunt, we took a shortcut by crossing through the baseball field on the way to the

Warner place on Lupine Road. Mrs. Warner, like clockwork, was always outdoors tending to her beautiful flowers. We recognized her by the shocking red hair and the tight yellow shorts that gave us a wonderful view of her round behind. "Boy, Ben, she's really pretty," Kenny said as he stared at the figure bending down to our right. I simply smiled and said, "Yeah." She probably spent half her day outside in the yard. But why not—that garden was an unequaled showcase. The lawn reminded me of a tiny golf course. I was afraid to walk over it; my sneakers might ruin its beauty. Of course that wouldn't have been an option, anyway.

As we passed by the green-and-white house on the way toward Elliott Street, I tried to guess where the Warner sisters were. Was Wanda inside practicing her piano lesson or attending dance class? Where was Elaine? The younger sister could've been doing anything. Whenever I stood on Lupine Road, I thought about Wanda or Elaine. Usually Wanda. I didn't know why but they became ingrained in my mind. Was this an early indication that I liked girls? It was like being in a trance, this giddy feeling. I didn't understand it.

When we reached the last house on Lupine Road before the main street I said, "I bet today Mr. Ellison gives me the biggest pickle."

"No, he likes me better," my friend snapped back, grinning. "He'll pull a whopper out of the jar for me." He held out his hand and we shook on it.

"You wait and see, buddy, I know I'm right," I bragged.

Kenny retorted by pushing me a little. "No way, I'm always right."

We took a left on Elliott Street and went about a fourth of a mile up past Danny's house and then the whole purpose of the afternoon was upon us. Climbing some wooden stairs we entered Ellison's Grocery, where a wonderland of goodies greeted the customer. Many kids frequented this store, which carried everything from assorted candies to choice meats and vegetables. The corner store was the rule in those days, not an exception. There were the omnipresent First National and A and P, large markets where women went to shop for their family needs. But a kid's excitement came from a small establishment like Ellison's and Amero's Variety, which was directly across the street. Some people favored Ellison's while others preferred Amero's. A few kids went to both stores. But each place did a thriving business in spite of their competitive closeness. And everybody got along. It wasn't as if it were one side against the other. Kenny and I loved Ellison's. That didn't mean that Blubberguts resented us for not going to his father's store. We were still good friends and teammates. Mr. Amero's biggest concern was his robust son's gobbling up of several goodies. I never forgot the day that Larry Buccini, Blubberguts' best friend, whispered to me one day in front of Ellison's. "Hey, you know what, Ben? Blubberguts told me he got spanked hard for having too many candy bars, around five at one time. His father caught him while sneaking a look from the back room." Even though I felt sorry for Blubberguts, I couldn't restrain myself and roared.

Blubberguts had done it again and abused his quota for the day. What was that, a hundred pounds of stuff? Plainly, he was becoming a fat pig, but one who could really belt the ball to smithereens.

When Mr. Ellison, a tall, string bean of a man saw Kenny and me standing in front of him, he didn't say a word but the blank stare on his face said it all. I always felt sorry for the guy because he was perpetually in a bad mood. A lot of the kids were afraid of him and called him names, like the "crank." Most everyone in the neighborhood had heard about his mysterious accident. He had a wooden leg, the left one, as a result of some childhood mishap. How this unfortunate thing had befallen the miserable fellow, no one was certain. But there was a noticeable limp, accompanied by a hint of pain. The fact, however, that he had a pretty wife who was always smiling was his redemption.

He went over to the famous pickle jar that stood on the main counter and contained many sour pickles. To say that this seemingly unimportant action on the part of the storeowner was important to us was a gigantic understatement. I could practically taste the acid mixing with the saliva in my mouth, as if I'd already sucked the juice out of a pickle. Kenny poked me in the stomach and murmured, "I can't wait. You wait and see, I'm going to win." It was a noteworthy symbol of our being buddies, these pickles were. We stood there impatiently and watched for Mr. Ellison to seal the deal. Finally, Mr. Ellison waved a large fork, then plunged it into the large jar and easily managed to liberate two pickles. Using a strip of brown paper, he passed them along as the smell of vinegar wafted over us.

We grabbed the pickles and I could see that Kenny was eager to see whose was the largest. My mouth watered and, to be honest, I didn't give a hoot if I were the winner or not.

"That'll be a nickel, boys," he said, without smiling. That was one thing about good old Mr. Ellison. Everything with him was simply business.

We each handed him a nickel and walked over to the candy counter. As usual, he didn't say thank you when we paid him. He was rigid, automatic in his dealings with all his customers. Anything different would've seemed out of line, strange.

"See, I told you I'd win," Kenny said, sticking his pickle in front of my face. "You're lucky," I said.

Chewing on our pickles we went over to the candy counter, which jolted the buyer as soon as he entered the store. We stared at the countless candy bars along with numerous novelties to munch on that covered three shelves, all purposely arranged to entice any kid into making a purchase. Many candies were a penny each. No one ever entered Ellison's Grocery without leaving a nickel or two poorer. Nobody cared. Our parents didn't go broke over the purchase of some sweets. If anyone lacked the right amount of change, it wasn't beyond the realm of reason that he could borrow the money from a friend. Whether any kid took advantage of another was a possibility. But such an awful fate was the fault of the innocent victim, not the responsibility of the creep who'd committed such an awful deed. That's where the duty of the parents came in. Instead of squealing to your parents, you attempted to settle the matter between the two of you. In this regard Kenny and I didn't have a problem. Both of us fortunately were supplied with an adequate amount of jingling coins. That's why we never got into a fight over it. "Hey, Kenny, did you hear that Big Billy Grant bummed a nickel off of Sally Lorenzo? I can't believe it. You know he'll never pay her back."

"She must be stupid, if you ask me. Just like a silly girl," Kenny said sarcastically.

Our buying any candy at such a time was out of the question. It spoiled the whole concept of sour pickle time. How could anyone of a sane mind combine a pickle with something sweet? Kenny and I were cheap, anyway. We were scrounges of the first magnitude. We never parted with our money, except for the pickles. It wasn't as if we had a million bucks to squander. My father took me into his office twice a week and lectured me on many things. I got fed up with constantly being told how to act in every situation. "Look, Ben," he emphasized, his arms folded. "I worked hard for my money. Understand that it never comes easy. I want you to be careful, not to spend it carelessly on just anything. Understand?" I nodded. "Good," he smiled. "Also, I don't want you to hang around with just anyone. Choose your friends wisely. It'll make a big difference in your life. You see?" Dad never wore a tie and shirt anywhere, even at work. This always puzzled me because my brothers and I always had to wear a tie and sport coat whenever we attended church. Once Dad confided in me that the Rotary Club had fined him five dollars for having the temerity of attending a meeting with a tie on.

On game day, after the East Danvers Red Sox had crushed another opponent, my father would treat the team. Each player was entitled to one candy bar and one can of soda pop. It always gave me a weird feeling inside, knowing my father was doing this charitable thing. In a way it made me the center of attention, which I loathed. My father's generosity put me on display. I didn't want the kids to think that I thought I was better than they were. Did they believe this? I hoped not. I always chose a Charleston Chew and Orange Crush. Without fail, that was my decision. Kenny, on the other hand, differed each time. One time he picked a Milky Way and a root beer. Other times he went for Three Musketeers and orangeade. What all this cost my father was beyond my comprehension. It bothered me, but I figured he must've been able to afford it.

We left Ellison's and headed back down Elliott Street. For an hour or so, we wandered about aimlessly, sucking and biting on our pickles. It was one of the greatest times in my life because it was a time when I loved doing what I was doing—yet I didn't understand why.

My grandmother was sitting at the kitchen table and cutting fresh green beans. She was forever busy doing something, as if by stopping she'd cease existing. Was this the only reason for her being there in the first place? I wondered. Nanny was in her late seventies but looked much older than that. Her hands were noticeable in that they were covered with brown spots and appeared very rough and dry, badly in need of some hand lotion. They were probably the most-used hands in the world. Her face was puffy and very white. I never recollected her ever going outside in the sun. Her hair was white and getting thinner each day. She wore a long, drab-looking dress that reached to her black shoes. She'd taken care of two sons and a daughter and, most importantly, a spoiled husband for many, many years. Perhaps her family would've died had she not stepped in to assist them in the daily rituals of life. Shameful to say I guessed that not one of them were ever cognizant of this. It was a fact of life and taken for granted.

I was standing in the middle of the kitchen not far from the pantry. "Please sit down, Ben," she said quietly. "I want to tell you a scary tale."

It was just weeks into Kenny's and my pickle-eating phase. Since Nanny was my mother's mother and the only grandma I knew, I listened intently. She could be unbelievably strict, but I loved her dearly because I realized she only criticized me for my own good—plus I had too much respect for her to argue any point discussed. She'd grown up in the small town of Wolfeboro, New Hampshire, in a community rampant with rumors. And she'd recently heard of my fascination with pickles.

This story remained with me all through my early years. Whenever I took a jaunt with Kenny to Ellison's I thought about what I'd heard.

"I want you to know how dangerous pickles are for you," Nanny said, stopping what she was doing and looking directly at me. I was taken back by what she'd said. "Yes, Ben, that's right. Way back when I was a little girl, long, long ago in another era—I know you can't believe I was once young—I had a grammar school friend, a boy about my age, who loved pickles probably as much as you do now. He couldn't stop eating them. From the grapevine, and Arthur eventually told me the story himself, apparently one day he outdid himself and ate more than his allotted share of the green things. His parents panicked and called in their physician, one of only two in town. According to a reliable source Arthur had had difficulty gaining weight. He'd eaten pickles since his early childhood on. Imagine that, Ben! After investigating Arthur's case, Dr. Osgood, who was our doctor too, surmised that his patient's blood was weak. It was determined that all the juice in the pickles that had passed through his body was the culprit. So you see," Nanny stressed, pointing her finger at me, driving her point home. "My young friend stopped his outrageous habit and gave up pickles altogether. Alas, from then on, his life became normal and all was well."

Had this really happened or was it a part of Nanny's imagination? Whatever, it affected me greatly. Being so close to Kenny I had to tell him. "Do you believe what happened to that kid in New Hampshire?" I asked. "It's incredible if it's true." We were descending Cardinal Road on the way to Ellison's for another pickle. "C'mon, be serious, Ben. Are you crazy or something?" It was late in the summer and Kenny had on red shorts that exposed muscular legs that had been transformed into a dark brown color by the sun. He'd just had another short haircut and never wore a cap to protect his head from the heat. His thick, jet- black hair protected him from getting sunstroke, or so he claimed. As we finished our short trip, I understood that Kenny wasn't as gullible as I was, so he couldn't have cared less about Nanny's story.

A contradiction existed as far as Kenny and I were concerned. Sometimes I preferred to be with him; other times, I didn't. Whenever I was with someone, I reasoned, I was never totally myself. With him, I was as much of myself as was humanly possible for me to be with another person. He was fun to be with. When alone, I was one hundred percent myself. No one was present to interfere with my thoughts or actions.

Furthermore, with Scott sometimes around to get in the way of anything that I might be doing at the time I was a very small percentage of my potential self. After all, he was named after my father. Therefore, I surrendered to his superiority in all matters. I thought, correctly I believed, that to confront the staggering odds in anything involving my older brother was futile. It was a no-win situation. The winner was predetermined, as was the loser. The only trait I'd inherited that surpassed Scott's was that my grades were always higher. But so what?

One lazy afternoon, about an hour after school had let out, I was sitting in the living room when Mom appeared. Most of the week it had rained hard but the sun had managed sporadically to reappear. It was for me the slowest part of the day, what I thought of as "hanging around" time. In three hours it would be suppertime.

My mother, dressed casually in a green sleeveless blouse and a dark brown skirt that came below her knees, walked into the room. She had just returned from food shopping. The curtains were open, causing a brilliant light to enter the room. Mom had light brown hair that almost reached to her shoulders. Her face's angular features, especially her marvelous cheekbones and high forehead, hinted to an insightful observer that she could've pursued many other avenues other than motherhood. Maybe even an actress. I always considered her to be a beautiful woman. Her figure was just right; her proportions often invited other men to steal a glance (much later on, during my only trip to Florida with my parents, Don Cornell, the famous crooner, came up to her while singing a song). However, Mom never seemed to be aware of others' adoration of her. She was modest and polite to a fault.

"I think this is a wonderful time for us to have a chat," she said, sitting down on the couch.

"Why, have I done something wrong?" I asked.

"Of course not, Ben. What makes you say that?" She quickly got up and came over to me and kissed me on the forehead. "All three of you boys are wonderful kids, you as much as Scott and Andy. You know that, don't you?" She took my hand and escorted me back to the couch. "Sit here with me, okay?

"I've noticed lately, sweetie, that something is bothering you. Am I right? Sometimes you mope around the house as if you aren't happy. That's what I'm here for, to help you. It bothers me a lot whenever any of my boys seem down."

I looked away from her and wanted to cry, but I didn't. "I'm not as good as Scott in anything. I'm a jerk. Nothing goes right."

"That's not true, Ben. Stop feeling sorry for yourself. Haven't I told you that? C'mon." Mom was getting angry. "You're simply wrong, that's all. For goodness sake, you have Kenny as your best friend, you can play ball and you're very smart in school."

"Yes, but Scott is much better than me in everything. I'll never hit a home run or pitch the way he can."

My mother put her arms around me and kissed me again, this time on the cheek. "Yes, it's true that Scott can do some things better than you, but don't you understand that it's only natural that some people have more abilities than others. You get much better grades than Scott, don't you?"

I began to smile. "Yes, I think so, Mom. But nobody cares about that. They only go by how good you are in sports."

"Yes, sweetie, some people do—but not everyone. I care very much how well you do in your subjects just as much as how far Scott can hit the ball. Maybe more." She patted me on the shoulder. "You must realize, Ben, that Scott might someday be a star in baseball and football. But so what? You should be proud of that, just like he should be happy if you're good in the classroom. You have to think you're as smart and good as anyone," she stressed. "You, Ben, can't go around every day thinking you aren't as good as your brother and mustn't worry about what others think of you. If you do that, you'll be miserable all the time. You know I grew up with two older brothers, don't you? Your Uncle Bennie is a couple years younger than Uncle Artie and he was always in the same shoes as you are now. He wasn't as good in sports as your Uncle Artie was and he turned out just fine. You understand?"

"Yes, Mom, I think so."

I attempted to convince myself that my mother was correct in her thinking. What else could I do? I did, however, have a far different view of things. Who cared about my intelligence, my overall performance in school? No one did, as far as I was concerned. What was on top of the list centered on my image and I was afraid, for some stupid reason, to try my hardest. I never went all out when I played for the East Danvers Red Sox. I allowed Scott to be in the spotlight. Instead, I displayed how weak I was to the world. Consequently, I was average. A price was to be paid if you didn't excel in front of your peers. I did, unfortunately, care too much what other people thought of me. I had to hold my own, like Scott did. He not only held his own, he ruled the universe around him. After my conversation with my mother, I was determined to express myself in a more confident manner. I kept telling myself to do that. Yes, I had to work hard on it. Fortified with Mom's talk, I felt better about things. Maybe it was achievable, maybe it wasn't. With that frame of mind I went forward.

CHAPTER FIVE

There was the story of "the clappers." It originated out of nowhere and developed a force all its own. It lasted for the duration of an entire summer and into the fall. And it became a vehicle used effectively by four of us kids. Joey and Scott versus Kenny and me in a competitive match that, at times, became a bit nasty. It was a rare opportunity for me to outshine my older brother. I relished the very strength it gave me. Scott chose Joey as his partner only because he knew he could control him.

Up the hill from Lupine Road diagonally across from the very top about ninety yards from our ball field stood a house of brick and wood. Not a complete house, but a half-finished one that seemed to take years to develop. So if Ted Williams, the Splendid Splinter, were to stand at our home plate and take a ferocious cut at the ball with his famous swing, it would land directly in the interior of that roofless structure. A great blast, but attainable for someone of his stature. What an unforgettable sight it would be.

There was something uneven about the house, something out of kilter. Bricks, old and new, of different shades of red, jutted out every which way: Half a wall here, a completed one there. Maybe the man building it had something in mind that I couldn't see. Something that made his future place stand out, and caused a stir in the solidly traditional community. Just his presence as the new guy on the hill had already accomplished that. He was a big fellow who wore a sleeveless dungaree shirt. Muscular arms forced themselves out of the denim material, which made him appear even larger. Many times Kenny and I had stood nearby in the roadway admiring his hard work. To us, building that house with its twists and turns was a seemingly insurmountable task.

His departure time each evening varied. Once, after the mystery man had left around five-thirty, Kenny and I went snooping around. Nothing could possibly come of it. We were two innocent boys in search of something exciting. Numerous times I'd recalled Dad's warning me about exploring places that could be deemed dangerous. "Ben, don't ever do things alone or with Kenny that can get you in trouble. You never know what can happen to you." He was the last person on earth who should've been preaching to me. Had he been in my situation with Kenny at that very moment he would've jumped in without hesitating. Dad's incident with the frog proved that. "My father would never think this is dangerous, Kenny, would he? We're doing nothing wrong here. If he considers this a bad move he's dead wrong," I emphasized. "Yes, Ben, you're right," Kenny offered. "Let's get busy. Stop worrying about it. He'll never know about it."

My body was shaking as we approached our destination. Certainly no one had given us permission to trespass on this man's land. I thought that we were committing a crime. The closer we got to the house, the guiltier I felt.

The whole area was a mess. Several half-filled wheelbarrows were scattered about, tilting in odd ways. I suddenly bumped against one I hadn't noticed, and fell to the ground. My knee hurt but I didn't let Kenny know that anything was wrong. It was a sign, I thought, that we never should've come to this stupid place.

"I don't think we should be here," I said. "We should go back."

"Don't be crazy, Ben. It's a great idea." Kenny's thin face showed the beginnings of a smirk.

"No, I don't think it is."

"Let's go inspect the inside," Kenny said, walking over to the house to climb over the lowest part of the wall.

I tried again. "My father's going to be angry."

"That's nuts, Ben. We're not doing anything wrong here." Kenny was inside by then. He kept looking back to make sure I was following his lead.

My stomach ached with guilt and my knee pounded. I didn't want to check if it were bleeding. Would that have made a difference? "It's supper time. My mother's going to wonder where I am."

"Stop worrying about everything," he yelled. "This is fun."

"My father's back from work."

"So what? So he's back from work. My dad probably is too."

"Okay," I said. "We'll stay a while." I felt my shoulders slump as I trailed after my friend.

"Great," he said, his voice sounding victorious.

That was my biggest problem. I constantly fretted over my father. Would he approve of this or that? Would Mom take my side of an issue if Dad wouldn't? Back and forth it went. I was a loony bin. I always believed that Scott and my father were in cahoots, that they had an agreement between them. There was a bonding there that no one could separate, least of all, me. By nature I had been placed into a situation from which I would never escape. What could be done to deal with it? The only two people on my side were my mother and my grandfather. Mom went out of her way to console or counsel me whenever the occasion called for it, and there were many such times. The only problem with her helping me was that it brought on another major obstacle. I became furious. I fully realized that she was sympathetic in her feelings toward me. But I also knew that she tried to hide that very fact from my father. Was she actually afraid of him? I pondered this for a long time. He was never present at the exact moment she was there for me. Was she hiding the fact of whose side she was really on?

I suspected all along he knew how she treated me, that she favored me over Scott. This, in turn forced Dad, out of necessity, to support even further his namesake. Scott, Jr. was the darling of Scott, Sr. I never knew how Scott felt about this.

Dusk began to fall and my stomach was turning into

knots. "Kenny," I said, pulling on his sleeve. "We have to get out of here."

Kenny kept walking through each darkened room as if he didn't hear me.

"Kenny," my voice went from insistent to a complaining bleat. "My dad's going to cream me if we stay here any longer."

Tossing his head with a swagger I envied and despised, Kenny said, "My dad trusts me. I can stay however long I want." He pushed his hands out as if he were swatting at a fly. "Go if you want." Then he did really smirk. "I won't tell."

I figured it was around six-thirty. My supper was long gone. Everyone in the family had eaten and my father was probably steaming inside. The punishing factor was a certainty. This I felt in my heart, and sooner I knew I'd feel some other place on my body as well. Whenever it reached this particular stage where I was aware that I was facing punishment, I became the martyr. I complained silently. How could this be happening to me? It never happened to anyone else. It was definitely Kenny's fault.

My knee pained me. When I pulled the pant leg of my dungarees up, I could see a little blood that had dried. This meant that I was now doubly terrified of how my father would react. I'd be lucky to survive his ranting, not to mention that my mother would be powerless in my predicament. She always agreed with Dad when he lost his temper; there was no way out.

A comforting breeze swept over the top of the hill. It was cool for this time of the year.

"I think my father's called your father."

"Yeah, I think so," Kenny said, still undeterred.

"We better get out of here, Kenny. Okay?"

"Yeah, you're right, Ben. Maybe my parents are getting concerned by now."

We started to exit the house.

"What's this?" he wondered, picking up a wooden block positioned on the ground. Many more of them were strewn throughout the place. "Wow, these things are interesting, Ben." He went over and picked up a half dozen or so of the blocks, cradling them in his arms. "Here, take some of these," he ordered. "We maybe can use them later on. Let's get out of here." His face suddenly displayed a scowling expression, something I wasn't used to seeing. He seemed nervous and started mumbling to himself. Kenny was always intrigued about things he came upon unexpectedly. He was an inquisitive kid who was able to think up possible games with just about anything. I wondered what in the devil he'd do with these blocks.

"What's wrong?" I inquired, picking up two blocks and smacking them together, one against the other. "We're wasting time, Kenny."

Kenny looked at me and said, "Wow, what a great sound! I never heard that noise before."

"Yeah, it's a great sound." Just to go along with my friend, I hit the blocks together again, making a clapping sound. It was satisfying in a way that I couldn't really understand.

Upon our arriving at his house he whispered to me, "Let's

go around the back and hide these blocks in the cellar. I don't want my father to see them, okay? It won't take long, then you can go home." At this point I was angry. "It doesn't make any difference now. It's too late. I'm in for it," I moaned.

When I finally reached Twenty Hillcrest Road I attempted to avoid everyone by sneaking around the back door and tiptoeing through the small den. Any success I might have hoped for was thwarted as I passed through the kitchen on the way to my room. Unfortunately I didn't see my mother standing in the corner of the kitchen by the refrigerator. Her shadow was imprinted on the wall. Her arms were folded as she stared at me. I was stunned as I looked out of the corner of my eyes. There was nothing I could've uttered at this instant that would've made any sense. But anything was worth a try.

"I bumped my knee, Mom," I said, looking at her. "Right here," I added. "It hurts when I touch it."

There was one thing about my mother that was absolutely splendid. She was a compassionate person. And I, more than Scott and Andy combined, clearly understood her reaction toward any erratic behavior. As I stood there with my pant leg pulled up to my thigh to display my war-like wound, I saw a slight smile come over her face. It wasn't a wide smile, but one that was trying to comprehend my dilemma.

"See, Mom, right here. It's bleeding." I began to rub my knee.

"Leave it alone," she said. "Okay, I see it." She came over

to me and examined the sore. "I think you'll make it through the night, Ben. I'll put some Mercurochrome on it."

"Mom," I responded, beginning to plead with her. "I'm sorry I'm late. I was with Kenny. He wouldn't let me come home."

"I figured that out for myself, Ben," she said. "And don't make any excuses for yourself or Kenny. He didn't make you do anything. Don't you know how worried about you I was?"

"Yes, Mom."

She hugged me tightly. "Now go to your room and I'll bring you your supper."

"Okay, Mom."

I turned around and headed directly for the hallway.

My father stood right there in the doorway. I never forgot the intensity of that glare!

"Ben, I want you to come with me to your room. Straight ahead, young man," he asserted. He led me down the hall to my bedroom on the left. I could hear my mother crying a short distance away; I felt badly for her.

Upon entering the room Dad sternly said, "Take off your dungarees and lie face down on your bed. Leave your underpants on." I quickly removed my pants and did as I was told. My fingers became numb and my stomach felt queasy. I shook inside. Besides that, I hadn't had anything to eat since noontime.

"Now stay there and I'll be right back," he ordered. "Don't move, do you understand?"

"Yes, Dad." I wanted to cry, but I didn't.

I didn't know where he'd gone but moments later he returned. My heart was beating so fast that I actually lost my bearings. I didn't know where I was.

Dad began whacking me on my behind with something hard which I couldn't see because of my prone position. To say that it hurt didn't do it justice. It stung more with each blow; I lost count after the first two.

When the episode was over, I got up slowly, tears in my eyes. Somehow, though, I refused to speak to him. I was so upset I couldn't even look at my father. I still heard my mother crying somewhere, which bothered me tremendously. I wanted to call out for her but realized it was out of the question. I yearned to be with her.

When Dad was gone I quickly shut the bedroom door and wept like I never had before. Up until then I had tried not to break under all the pressure, an almost impossible task. I felt a little better about myself because I theorized I had taken it like a man as my father had always instructed me to and perhaps I'd deserved such a fate. I guessed the whole punishment routine had lasted about five minutes.

I honestly didn't know whether my silence had bothered him, but I was hoping it had. It gave me a great sense of relief when the idea of his suffering a bit through this brutal incident entered my mind. I found out later that he'd used a thick cribbage board on me. I wondered several times if Dad possessed a cruel streak. I often questioned his bouts of anger, his methods of punishing me. Did that go for Scott and Andy too? I didn't know. Was it fear or respect that I felt? Much later on I surmised he was full of conflicting emotions. I learned one important thing, however, from having been treated so severely. I was forever sickened by the very thought of anyone's being physically disciplined. Maybe for some it worked. For me, it didn't.

Several minutes later my mother came into my room with a tray of food. It was one of my favorite meals, spaghetti and meatballs. No one made it quite like she did. I could smell the onions that were mixed in with Mueller's thin spaghetti, whole tomatoes, peppers, ground beef and a variety of spices. Having this treat at a time like this assuaged my intense feelings. Cold milk and chocolate cake topped off the supper.

She had tears in her swollen eyes and kept looking around to see if my father were nearby. In essence I thought she was sort of sneaking the meal my way, knowing all too well that my father would be dead set against her consoling me if he became aware of it. Mom appeared pleased that she didn't spot him.

She forced a smile and offered, " Here, Ben. I'm so glad that's over with. Are you okay?" She looked me over. "Sweetie, you look fine," she sighed, taking a deep breath and seeming to be somewhat relieved. "Please don't think of your father as being a bad guy. He doesn't mean to hurt you."

I appreciated and loved Mom's attempt at trying to make me feel better. However, I remained quiet because I was still seething inside and swore I'd never forgive Dad for what he'd done. I did feel greatly comforted by my mother's gallant effort.

In the event he might suddenly appear out of nowhere, I gobbled down the stuff as if it were my Last Supper on planet Earth.

CHAPTER SIX

Seldom did it happen, but when it did, it affected the East Danvers Red Sox. The whole team, excluding Scott, became quickly discouraged. One boy whined about the handling of a play or the unfair treatment he was receiving. He stormed off the field and headed home. That left us with an unbalanced game, an odd number of participants. What transpired then was nothing short of a miracle. This was Scott's chance to show off his amazing talent as a true leader. How he actually accomplished such a feat didn't surprise me at all. He didn't seem to care what anyone thought of him. Even though he probably knew that some members of the team hated his guts, he always assumed a so-what attitude. That's how outrageously sure of himself he was.

Scott made it appear as if the disgruntled player were at fault. He was the big jerk in the group, the ratty kid who should be looked down upon for having taken off like that. How dare he challenge Scott, go against the general good of the team? He left right in the middle of the game. Scott made it clear that this guy was a quitter, wasn't a good representative of the East Danvers Red Sox.

"I'm not going to play," Blubberguts yelled, throwing

down a bat and retrieving his glove. "It's not fun, anymore."

On the morning that Blubberguts the loser ran off in disgust, the rest of the game lasted only ten minutes. The morale of the kids had been fractured. Scott figured this out soon enough. He was a manipulator. Camouflaging his rare failure to control the situation, Scott fooled everyone except me. I could easily read through his ruse, his false pronouncement that he had to attend to something. This action was most unusual, especially in the middle of the morning.

"That's okay, guys, we don't need him," Scott said, waving at Blubberguts as he descended Cardinal Road. "Let him go, he's not that good, anyway." He gestured toward Andy and me to leave with him. "I have to help Mom with something." That was all it took for the game to end.

Andy and I followed our older brother home. Crossing Hillcrest Road, we were greeted on our front lawn by our dog, Pepper. He was a big black mongrel that resembled a Retriever. I spent a lot of time lying beside him on the floor in our living room and kissing his head. He was always there for me. His tail in constant motion told the whole story. I inherited a love of animals from my mother, who often described the loyalty of animals to anyone willing to listen and insisted that they were innocent creatures of God. According to her, no animal was ever to blame for biting or snapping at a human being. It was the person's fault for provoking the poor thing in the first place.

It should be known by any East Danvers person interested in this period that the classic fights between Newmar and Pepper should be recorded in the official documents of the town under the "animal" category. The property of the Warner family, Newmar was a mean-looking critter, a large, rusty-colored dog that often roamed around the right field area near the Warner house, even as we were in the process of playing. Oh, he was perfectly friendly toward us kids. In fact, he was downright lovable at times. He often chased after the ball. A few of us loved patting the bountiful coat of hair that covered his thick body. He reciprocated in kind, often lapping and slurping at our fingers. This diversion irritated Scott no end. It was interrupting the game. Newmar carried no grudge against the East Danvers Red Sox. We were confident he was rooting for us. And when he was by his lonesome, we were rooting for him. Then Pepper showed up.

When Pepper, our big black dog and the pride of the family, spotted Newmar, he raced straight down the hill in pursuit of his only adversary in the neighborhood. He headed past third base, then second base, until he was almost upon Newmar. He stopped just short of his intended mark. He was preparing for what was to ensue. Newmar, likewise, seemed to hesitate, then retreated. The two dogs, with their hair standing on end, waited. As for us kids, one thing became clear. We feared for the safety of both animals. Nonetheless, sides were taken. Family counted. Did a kid cheer for Pepper or for Newmar? It depended. We Robblees understood the seriousness of this forthcoming canine scuffle. Undoubtedly it produced a clash between two decent families. My mother never would know how to react if she ran into Mrs. Warner. My father, unafraid of any conflict, would know what to do and by all accounts would welcome it. He'd confront Mr. Warner with no regard to diplomacy. A bad feeling between the two would develop which might drag on for months. My father didn't budge on any issue, unlike me. I worried and fretted over everything. What would Wanda or Elaine think? Would they blame me? My family? I really cared for the two girls and their opinions. They might hate me just because Newmar had been injured in a stupid fight with our Pepper. What would Wanda say to me when I ran into her? She'd probably walk away in disgust and never want to speak to me again. My level of confidence would sink to an all-time low.

This time the dogfight lasted for a couple of minutes. Thank goodness, Mrs. Warner, who was working in her garden not far away from us, had seen what was transpiring. Hoe-in-hand, she dashed forward waving the implement all the while and screaming, "Newmar!" Wilted flower petals fell off her green apron as she approached the growling dogs. "Stop it!" she yelled, her voice cracking. That brave action on her part prevented a major catastrophe. It was a masterful effort. Each dog somehow succeeded in getting in a couple of bites. Other than that, nothing harmful came of it. Newmar had listened obediently to his owner and seemed unscathed. Pepper was all right, too. I felt so much better, as if I had been the one fighting and had escaped with no gaping wounds. I was truly thankful that a sensible adult had stepped into the fray. Good for her, I thought. What a great lady. Now I didn't have to worry about what the Warner sisters would think of me since they in all likelihood would never even hear about the dogfight. They were always busy in other matters. My brothers and I didn't inform our parents. Sometimes it was better to leave well enough alone. My mother would've been too upset over Pepper, anyway. Who knows what my father would've done. We didn't want to chance it.

CHAPTER SEVEN

One Wednesday in mid August Kenny and I met Scott and Joey at the field. We weren't going to play baseball that particular morning. As had been his custom, Scott had let the kids in on the news after our game on Tuesday. What the boss dictated, we followed. By the huge smiles on everyone's sunburned face, I knew the guys were elated they were getting a whole day off to themselves. They had twenty-four hours of freedom from Scott. Who were the East Danvers Red Sox, anyway, a Major League team with all those stupid rules? The most amazing thing was that no kid dared to go home and tell his parents of Scott's strictness. A chain reaction would've resulted with the shamed member facing unbearable ridicule in front of everyone. It wasn't worth it.

Kenny had asked me the evening before to come to his house as early as possible. That morning he handed me an armful of the clappers.

He said in a thrilled, conspiratorial-sounding voice, "We have to take these out of the cellar before my parents see them." I lifted them, smelling their woody scent.

When Scott saw all those wooden blocks, he started to pace, so I knew he was irritated. "What are they for?" he asked, as if we were trying to smuggle something valuable and secretive onto the field.

I shrugged and dropped my clappers at home plate. Kenny made a great show of putting each piece of wood down one at a time, as if they were made of gold. This bothered my brother even more, and his pacing increased.

Kenny pointed and said, "These clappers are all over the place up there at that house."

I took a quick breath and thought my friend was stepping on delicate ground.

"Why not," Kenny suggested to Scott, "invent some kind of game, something that would be competitive, using these clappers? Wouldn't that be a great idea?"

I was getting a kick out of this. Kenny was trying to rile Scott and was almost succeeding.

Scott picked up one of the pieces of wood, then another. He hit them together, causing the same sound as before. He asked, "Kenny, what can be done with these things? Are you out of your mind or something?"

Kenny shook his head and shot back, "No, why did you say that?" I could tell that Scott was becoming angry. My buddy turned toward me for some needed support. What I proceeded to do surprised even myself.

I suggested to Scott and Joey, who was standing there like a dummy beside his partner, "Let's try to imagine different codes with the clappers. Certain combinations of bangs will represent signs or places or distances in the neighborhood."

Joey stood there like the jerky kid he was. Even Scott couldn't understand what I was describing. I didn't let them know that Kenny had devised the intricacies of these codes the very day of our discovery. He had actually developed an entire system using those blocks. For instance, two bangs followed by three bangs indicated a certain location, such as the Cappadonna house down the hill on Cardinal Road. Four more bangs meant one of us was behind the fence on that same property. The idea was for Scott and Joey to find Kenny and me as soon as they could. And we would be looking for them at the same time. Kenny and I would signal each other as to one another's whereabouts. We had to find stations near each other, but in different locations. The more codes we could dream up, the more hiding places we were able to have. To be honest, Kenny and I were much smarter than they were. Kenny had concocted an elaborate scheme too complicated for them. We used around twenty-five or thirty codes. In comparison Joey and Scott had only a half dozen or so codes.

When the day was done, since they didn't find us, we won. We had little trouble in finding them first. Our favorite spot of all was located near the elaborate flowers behind the tall hedges at the Warner place. That is, as long as Mrs. Warner wasn't outdoors working at the time. If she were gardening, as was usually the case, we headed for the half-finished building or for Joey's house, way down the hill from there. Everything depended on the slim chance that no one was present at any prescribed location at the time. The more deceptive we were in trying to find a place the better the outcome was. We never lost a game of hide-and-seek with those clappers. Scott was befuddled, Joey didn't know any better. Kenny and I ruled the world!

As the summer wore on, Kenny and I eventually lost interest in baseball. Scott probably did, also. Enough was enough. School was right around the corner. How long could anyone maintain an interest in any sport? Since each of us began playing and practicing and living as one of the East Danvers Red Sox, after a couple of months of virtually repeating the same rituals everyday, a change of pace was necessary. That's how I saw it. There still was one important game remaining with the Salem Witches.

My father informed me the Sorensen brothers ruled the upper Bridge Street section of Salem. The guys on the East Danvers Red Sox viewed Salem as a major city, a metropolis compared to the little town of Danvers. Likewise, the nearby cities of Peabody and Beverly were, to us, big places with big-deal people. Over there, in the Witch City, their athletic programs were superior, especially in football and basketball. Legendary in the eyes of people on the North Shore, the Salem-Beverly battle on Thanksgiving Day had no equal in the area. Crowds surpassing fifteen thousand jammed into the stadium to see one of the premier games in the state. And to stress the importance of Salem sports, wouldn't you know that my father was once a football and basketball player there. That's all I heard growing up. How great the mighty Witches had been. They still were. But the thing that stood out the most in my mind centered on my Uncle Artie. "He was such a wonderful player," Mom reminded me over and over again concerning her heralded brother. Artie had been a force as a great halfback beginning in 1920 at Salem High School, then in the early 20s at the University of New Hampshire and, finally, as a star for the Providence Steamrollers in the pros. He'd actually played against the immortal Red Grange and been the victor in that contest, 9-6, against the Chicago Bears. As I was maturing from a boy into a young man, I'd heard these oft-repeated stories of his exploits on the field of play. They became so amplified that my uncle became a sort of god in the history of my family. I relished the very idea that I was his nephew. If I could be just half as good as he was great, I'd do well.

My father's welding shop stood at the rear of one of Salem's main streets, right near the railroad track. Bordering the track was a makeshift ball field, if you wanted to call it one, composed of a little grass, some sprouting weeds, many stones, and loads of dirt. Whenever I visited the shop, which I tried not to do too often because my father would put me to work, I saw the Sorensen boys and the rest of their gang throwing the ball around and yelling foul epithets at each other. They all wore old clothes and were the dirtiest kids I'd ever seen. Because they had hung around Dad's shop since they were tykes, he'd practically adopted them. And he loved those boys much more than we realized.

The game with the Witches was scheduled for the Saturday before Labor Day. I was both sad and happy. It was to be the final time we'd be together as the East Danvers Red Sox. Another season of baseball was coming to a close, meaning no one knew what was ahead for the team the following year. Maybe it was the end of an era. How long does something that enjoyable last in the scheme of things? How many kids are handed, without their ever noticing it, such pure fun? Did we ever really appreciate it?

Danvers Park, where the old Twilight League and the junior high and high school teams performed, was the site of our big game. My father had arranged the affair for the middle of the morning. Our emotions were high. At about nine-thirty a red welding truck came screeching up right in back of the huge screen framing the diamond. Large black letters with THE ROBBLEE WELDING CO. were inscribed on both doors of the truck. It carried the entire Salem team. They were standing up in the back and showing their spirit as a team by yelling and smacking each other. All of us thought they were showoffs. What were they trying to prove? Leo, my father's handyman who did many odd jobs, was behind the wheel. His stringy white hair, mostly bald on top, and extremely weathered face made him look much older. Besides that, the poor guy was missing three or four front teeth, making his appearance comical. But he was one of the friendliest men I ever knew, forever smiling and joking with us. I could tell he didn't know what to make of the behavior of the Salem kids. They were probably laughing at the old man. During the cold winter months Leo drove one of my brothers or me on various errands. Taking a ride with the tobacco-chewing fellow in the front seat of his old Ford, the one with the hot heater directly in front of the passenger side, was an anticipated treat. Moist tobacco would be drooling from the corners of his mouth, which wasn't the prettiest sight I'd ever seen.

The Sorensen boys, who I guessed were about twelve and fourteen, not only were the real deal but also were rugged guys whose assertiveness surely aided their team. The older brother kept yelling encouragement to the other team members. "C'mon, let's murder them," he bellowed, pointing toward us. The one thing I noticed about their players from the very beginning centered on their combined hostility toward us. No one on the Salem side acknowledged any East Danvers Red Sox member. That bothered me, was very intimidating. "Gee, Ben," Kenny offered. "They act like real bad kids. They're not looking at us."

We began sizing up our opponents as we sat on the bench by the first base side. Their team was situated on the third base side. As I looked over, I noticed one boy spitting on the ground, quickly followed by another one doing the same repulsive thing, which caused my stomach to drop. I was uncomfortable to say the least; it was the first time I felt as if I were facing a true enemy head on.

As the East Danvers Red Sox took the field first, we didn't seem to have our accustomed zing. We were quieter, appeared concerned over the outcome of the game. Without fail our team always approached each contest with supreme confidence. The stunner was that even Scott said nothing as he stood silently on first base. Danny Doheney waited on the mound for the first batter to take his spot at the plate.

The Witches scored two quick runs off Danny in the top of the first inning, led by "Veal's" timely double to left center. Going by a name that caused much merriment on our side, Veal, I could tell by his physical presence, was much older than any kid playing that day. He had to be at least sixteen. What muscles he had. I figured out that the East Danvers Red Sox team was up against something sinister that wasn't fair. In fact, if push came to shove, it was obvious to me that Dad was pulling for the Salem boys. They were his kids away from home. I never told anyone what I thought, not even Kenny. It took me a long time to understand why my own father rooted for Salem. He had bought them their equipment, including sneakers and other items. It wasn't that he was a rich man; he was that generous. But I had to face the fact that they were from the wrong side of the tracks, which elicited Dad's compassion, plus he obviously could identify with them. My father had grown up in similar circumstances. He'd always had an affinity for youngsters living in a tough environment. They worked for what they got and we didn't. They weren't given anything; for them nothing was easy.

In the bottom of the first I was the leadoff hitter. Even though I was a bit nervous I took my place in the batter's box (I always had a straightaway stance). Waving my brown bat furiously over my right shoulder, a move that was probably the result of both habit and nervousness, I waited for the Salem pitcher's delivery. As I saw a swirling blur come directly my way, I did something that even surprised me. I suddenly squared around and laid down a perfect bunt! The baseball, which was brand new and completely white, unlike the ones we were accustomed to using while playing in East Danvers, rolled halfway down the first-base line—allowing me to easily reach base safely. It was perhaps the most delightful thing that I ever experienced in my career with the East Danvers Red Sox. As I stood on first base and looked over toward the Salem Witches' bench I noticed a slight grin on my father's face. It was one of the few times I felt I'd done a wonderful thing. Unfortunately, the next three batters—Kenny, Blubberguts, and Scott—were retired in order. I ended up on third base, thus wiping out my superb effort at the plate only minutes before.

Danny settled down after the first inning and pitched two more frames of perfect ball. Then it was Scott's turn to take over as the pitcher. He was now at center stage. Compared to our uneven, ragged field in East Danvers, the Twilight League one located in the Plains part of town was a professional venue. Clearly it was a privilege to be playing there. I couldn't imagine what it must've meant to the Salem kids.

With the score 2-1 in favor of Salem (it was the fourth inning), while our club was at bat, Scott suddenly changed his lethargic attitude and uttered, "What are we going to do, lose this game to these bums? You're kidding me. We're ten times better than them. Let's stop this crap and get going, guys. We can't lose our last game." He loomed in front of our whole team, who was sitting there on the bench looking up at him. "We aren't about to ruin our whole season, are we?" Scott started to clap his hands hard, which meant that he was taking complete control as he usually did. He was now pitching and, though he possessed extraordinary speed with every toss of the ball, he also was known for his wildness. Each opposing batter on Salem's team had to be alert on every single pitch lest his life was in danger. (Scott was forever erratic in his control as became evident in future years when he hurled for the high school nine).

The Witches scored three more times, as Scott walked seven batsmen over the last four innings. The man-child, Veal, smacked a single, a bullet of a short, right over the center of the mound. If Scott hadn't succeeded in ducking at exactly the right instant, he might've been seriously injured. Two of Veal's teammates scored, standing up. It was one of the few instances that I detected a scared look on my brother's face. The East Danvers Red Sox, when all was said and done, squeaked by, 6-5. Maybe it'd been a lesson for our team. We'd been real lucky. Of the twelve outs, Scott managed to fan ten batters. Most importantly, he slammed a three-run homer to deep left field that was the deciding factor. Only this time, thankfully, he didn't sound off. I always interpreted this as meaning that it was because our father was present. He didn't broadcast his spectacular feat to those who were present. He circled the bases, quietly and with dignity. I noticed my father standing in front of the Salem bench and clapping proudly at his son's achievement. It was something I was used to.

The most dramatic moment in the game erupted when Blubberguts, while rounding second base on his way to third, collided with Veal, the shortstop and his equal in stature. A fight ensued, with arms swinging, as Veal got the better of our guy. My father raced onto the field of play while screaming his brains out, "Stop it, boys."

I didn't know about the other kids, but I held it against my father for certain things that happened in that game. First of all, why did he spend the entire time with the Salem boys? He never came over to our bench to see how everything was going. I felt betrayed, a feeling that stuck with me for weeks. And Dad's allowing an older, stronger kid to go up against us was not only absurd but also dangerous. What if Blubberguts had been seriously injured? As big as he was, he never could've defended himself in a battle with that animal.

It was the final game ever played by the East Danvers Red Sox.

CHAPTER EIGHT

Joey Buccella was the most unique member of the East Danvers Red Sox. There was something innately mature about him that impressed me greatly. Kenny and I talked often about him. Many times I daydreamed that I was a good-looking Italian boy and possessed the same charm and know-how. For Joey, everything came easily and without a struggle, or so it seemed. He did things no one else dared to do. That was particularly true when it came to girls. If the girls at Williams School, or in our neighborhood, were polled, they'd all say that Joey was "cute," "a dream," or some other silly compliment. It was pure crap. No matter what the boys thought about Joey, it didn't seem to faze him, but I always got along well with him. He was that kind of kid. The girls liked him; they seemed to be attracted to him so much that they went looking for him.

Joey looked like he'd been in the sun for eternity. His skin was the color of light chocolate. His dark features were extreme. There were many Italian families living in East Danvers. It was no coincidence that as I got older, I was automatically drawn to Italian girls. That didn't mean they liked me. I imagined myself with them on a date. I couldn't help myself. That dark hair drove me crazy. As for Joey, he was the perfect Italian kid. The girls went bananas over him, something I simply couldn't fathom. The team picture of the East Danvers Red Sox was further proof that he stood out, looked like a foreigner. If a stranger were passing through East Danvers and ran into Joey he'd definitely believe he'd just seen a kid who'd gotten off the boat. The whole Buccella family had that dark skin. His sister Marie, I could tell, was going to be stunning when she got older. She was Andy's age and was the loudest kid within two miles. I heard her coming down Hillcrest Road with her friend Martha Grant, Little Billy's baby sister. The two girls were jabbering away so intently that I turned my head to see who was making such a racket. The thing was that Marie swaggered about with that same confident look that her brother Joey had passed along to her. And those vocal cords were inherited from her mother. There was no doubt about that. Mrs. Buccella's orders for her son "to come home right this minute" were legendary. As for Mr. Buccella, the kids on the East Danvers Red Sox were surprised if they saw him twice a year. Where was he? No one knew nor really cared.

There were a few girls who were either seeing Joey or flirting with him. It was apparent to me that one of them was the leading candidate to win his attention. She started hanging around the ball field. Scott made some demeaning comments to him but Joey didn't care. He just continued to play ball. Most of us thought that for a ten-year-old kid to be involved in any way whatsoever with a girl was ridiculous. But we never said a word to Joey. There was one characteristic about Joey that most of the kids were unaware of. They were too young to observe such a thing. He led people on, big time. I could see between the lines. I was average in sports but I prided myself in the matter of seeing through the actions of others. I was right on target about Joey. I wasn't a great athlete like my brother or Danny but I could think for myself. A person usually was who he thought he was. But I had to be honest with myself. That idea really didn't originate with me. It was Mr. Percy E. Foster, my brilliant grandfather, who let me in on some of the facts of life. I didn't deserve any of the credit at all. "Ben, never let anyone see you are weak," Bampy told me. "If you do, they'll take advantage of you and use you."

This pretty, brown-haired girl conspicuously showed up more and more at our morning practices to see Joey. We gave him some good-natured, teasing looks. Sometimes he would brag about it with some of us behind Scott's back He admitted that the girl who attended these sessions was two years older than he was, a fact that allowed him to rub it in a little. She was going into the seventh grade in the fall and her name was Barbara. I was waiting to see if Scott was going to really blow up.

Joey disappeared during the afternoon hours. He was never at home then. Whenever Kenny and I peeked from behind the shed at his grandmother's gruesome killing of the chickens, Joey was seldom around. At first we weren't even curious as to why. Then, as the summer progressed from late July into August, we wondered about our friend's whereabouts. Where could he be going? One afternoon, right after lunch, Kenny and I waited for him behind the shed. Joey, after only a few minutes, came out of the side door of his house and climbed up the hill leading to the incomplete brick house. The man working there was eating his lunch. Slowly stepping over the rough terrain, Joey walked down Lupine Road. "I don't think this is right, Kenny," I whispered. "We're being sneaky about this. It's like committing a crime, don't you think?" The two of us kept a safe distance behind Joey. "Yeah, I think it's wrong, too," Kenny said, " but it's a lot of fun. We're not hurting anyone, as far as I can see." Were we actually doing anything wrong? Following someone who was in a hurry wasn't an easy thing to do. What if he looked back and saw us? What would we do then? For a second there, I was wondering if he might be visiting one of the Warner girls. Did one of them like him? This thought made me uncomfortable. Didn't Elaine go for me? I suffered for a few seconds but was relieved when Joey went by the Warner house. He didn't even hesitate to look to see if they might be home. That was a close one, I thought.

Joey proceeded all the way down Elliott Street until he reached Williams School. Since it was level ground all the way, we never lost sight of him. We stayed around twenty-five or so yards behind, all the while holding our breath and hoping he wouldn't turn around and see us. He never did. His focus remained on where he was headed. At the school he took a sudden left turn, a side street off Elliott Street.

He was right next to the school. It was at that moment that we lost him. Joey, we guessed, disappeared into the second house on the street. How could we be sure where he was? I had a brainstorm. We walked quickly into the schoolyard, all the way over by the third-and-fourth-grade entrance, and sat on the swings that were located in the far corner by Elliott Street. From there we were able to keep an eye on the houses nearby, while pretending to be having innocent fun by ourselves. Joey, if he did spot us as he was coming out of one of the houses, never would've suspected a thing. How could he possibly think that his friends were trailing him? He wasn't smart enough to figure that out. Kenny and I were positive of that.

We swung back-and-forth for a good half-hour and waited. "Jeez, this is taking forever," I complained, getting up off the swing. "What're we suppose to do, wait here forever? It could take all afternoon and for what we know Joey maybe isn't in one of those cruddy houses. Maybe we're here for nothing, Kenny."

"Yeah, maybe you're right, that could be true. Let's wait a little longer. He's got to come out sometime," Kenny said. "Let's go over to those other swings, out of the sun. Boy, it's hot here. To leave now, Ben, is stupid. Let's relax, for crying out loud." There was a possibility that Joey had slipped out of the back door of the house where he was staying. Had our sneaky plan all been for nothing? We only wanted to find out about any girl he was seeing. Obviously we were too young and foolish to fully understand that we were intruding on our friend, the catcher on the East Danvers Red Sox. We continued to wait in the yard of Williams School; we had nothing more exciting to do.

At long last a brown-haired girl appeared at the front door of the corner house on the street. It was Barbara. The two of them came out, holding hands. Joey kept hold of Barbara's hand as they walked together down the other end of the street. Kenny and I weren't familiar with where they were going. By the time we'd crossed the school grounds and looked feverishly for them, it was too late. They had disappeared. We felt as if we'd been tricked. We were indeed fools for having done this. As we headed home, we fumed over what had transpired. "Do you believe this?" I cracked. "All of this was for nothing. How stupid can we be, Kenny? The joke is on us, buddy. All this time we thought we were playing a trick on poor Joey, when all along he really didn't even know about it and was making us look like the idiots we are. Now what do you think of our bird-brained scheme?" I inquired, slapping my sides.

"I have nothing to say, Ben," Kenny sighed, touching his face. "Let's get out of here and go home."

CHAPTER NINE

One day after playing a particularly sweaty game of baseball, Kenny said to me in a too-casual voice, "You want to go to Folly Hill?"

My stomach flopped. I wanted to shout yes and no to him at the same time. Yes because what kid didn't want to enter the wilds of Folly Hill, the only true wilderness in our town? But no because it was exactly that: wilderness. I envisioned all kinds of danger besetting my trusted friend and me: lions, tigers, and wild men who ate pre-adolescent baseball players for lunch, turned on a spit.

All the kids in East Danvers, at one time or another in their young lives, had a deep yearning to enter and explore the forbidden territory of Folly Hill, a distance of about a quarter mile from our house. To Kenny and me it was as if we were about to go on a safari to an African jungle. What was out there, we wondered. The closer a person got to the actual woods the more he was able to see the high hills and foreboding trees, along with the gigantic receptacle to the far left that served as a reservoir. Behind all that thick foliage in the forest lurked a world where any number of unknown horrors warned the curious traveler to beware.

Who had the ability to imagine what might happen to anyone brave enough to wander out to see for himself? That's the very excuse everyone used, why few ventured there unless accompanied by a friend, or better still, a bunch of kids. From within the confines of my quiet bedroom, I figured if I were to get murdered by a group of thugs, Kenny would be there alongside me to suffer a similar consequence. Our fates would be linked. When we gave it any thought, it was amazing how fearless a picture we presented to ourselves. Everything would be fine. But as we embarked on the actual event, our feelings of indestructibility faded fast.

We had to walk across an enormous field to reach our destination, which meant that we passed by several Vitelli Company trucks. It was about one in the afternoon. It wasn't as hot out as it had been the day before. This was good news to us. No one knew of our plans, including our parents. I told my mother we were, "just going out to play." My father wasn't home, meaning that there was nothing to be done around the house that day. My mother gave me permission and off we went.

There were half a dozen workers congregating around the Vitelli trucks. Two of them saw us but didn't say anything. They were dressed in sweatshirts, dungarees, and work boots. Kenny made a snide remark about their having to work so hard. After all, we didn't have to work at all. Except for a few chores we were free to do anything we wanted. We walked by them in quick order.

When we reached the obstructed entrance to the wooded

area, we climbed over a small stonewall, then entered Folly Hill. As we did so we realized it was official, we were inside the woods. I didn't know what Kenny was feeling but I felt both excited and queasy inside. It wasn't a bad feeling, yet it wasn't good, either. We had to go forward; it was too late to turn back. A worn pathway, suggesting there'd been many visitors here before us, lay ahead. There was an abundance of tall grass mixed with different kinds and colors of flowers on either side of the path. A steady buzzing sound dominated the space around us. I thought it might be crickets. I got closer to Kenny and announced, "There must be hundreds of bugs around here. Jeez, it's almost like being attacked or something. I feel weird, Kenny. You think they're flying and crawling everywhere?" Suddenly I felt uneasy, as if my body would have icky things all over it. Ever since I was real young I'd feared all kinds of tiny creatures that might invade me. Many times I'd dreamed about them. "Do you think there are any snakes here?" I added, looking around to make sure there weren't. Kenny, who was walking slowly just in front of me, answered, "Who knows. Maybe there are all kinds that bite people they don't like. Some probably sting like mad. I once saw a movie at the Paramount theatre in Salem with my whole family where a lot of people were dying from snakes and big red ants. One guy got eaten alive by millions of ants. He didn't have a chance, Ben." I believed Kenny enjoyed the fact that he was upsetting me; he wanted to see how far he could go. Being best buddies when it came to something between him and me, he still desired top billing in a situation like this. Kenny wanted me to rely on him. When he pulled that, it made me think of Scott and I became even more upset. Several years previous to that, while at Crane's Beach in Ipswich, I'd gotten lost for about an hour and my older brother finally was the one who'd found me. "Don't worry, Ben, you'll be all right," he'd assured me. "I'm here to protect you."

The first part of Folly Hill consisted of a lot of thick bushes, along with grass, weeds, and flowers. I saw a twig lying on the ground far away from a tree and called it "Mr. Lonely." Kenny spotted a bunch of weeds next to some flowers and referred to them as "The Ugly Ones." Once I started jumping up and down and waving my arms like the silly kid I was and yelled, "Giddy-up, Diamond," pretending I was on a horse, a lovely palomino. Kenny looked at me as if I'd lost my mind and said, "What a lunatic you are, you know that? You should be in Danvers State Hospital." Feeling insulted I replied, "You should talk."

My favorite shows, now that we Robblees had a new black-and-white television set, included Hopalong Cassidy, an impeccably dressed, white-haired, tough cowboy who hung around with his messy sidekick, the bearded Gabby Hayes, who was there for comic relief. There was the Lone Ranger with his famous horse, Silver; also the formidable Bob Steele, who always beat up his snarling foes, sometimes three outlaws at a time. "Kenny, I'll be the Lone Ranger and you be Tonto. I make a better Lone Ranger than you because I look at the show all the time and you look more like an Indian, anyway." He began to laugh and said, "Yes, I have much darker skin than you, buddy. Okay, I'll go along with you."

I realized as Kenny and I made our way deeper into the woods that my opportunity to explore with him in the future was running out. I wanted to stretch out my childhood for as long as I could. Unlike most kids who looked up to and aspired to be just like their parents, I wanted this to never end. I wanted to remain a child. But, somehow, I knew that it wasn't possible.

Up ahead was a large patch of prickly bushes bunched together. Appropriately, Kenny named it the Briar Patch. From behind it, we'd be able to hide and still be able to see the hills and slopes all around us. There was a huge open area straight ahead and after that loomed a steep hill resembling a small mountain. Yellow dandelions in the field gave us a delightful break from the heavier terrain we'd just left. There was both a beauty and a mystery about Folly Hill. We didn't know what was ahead over the hill. If we strained our eyes and gazed way over to the left, trying not to stare into the sun, we saw a large concrete reservoir. Many years later I found out that this had been constructed at the beginning of the Twentieth Century. Before that it'd been the exact location where a prosperous settler had built a mansion and lived with his family for many years.

Kenny pointed to an area ahead of us. We were still standing behind the Briar Patch. There was a figure moving about out there. The person was perhaps three-fourths of a football field away from us. The sun's brightness prevented us from seeing who it might be. But we were intrigued. We decided to wait to see where he was going. Then we'd follow him. We guessed it was a guy, mostly because it was highly improbable that it could be a girl. It would be silly if that were the case. How was a girl able to protect herself if she were alone in the woods? That would be worse than our being there. We figured that the girls at Williams School were much smarter than the boys were, anyway; they'd never wander aimlessly into the woods on their own.

Finally the figure ahead started to climb the hill about ten yards in front of him. It took him several minutes to accomplish that. We did nothing, choosing to stand still. He managed to finish climbing the hill. Then he disappeared over the horizon. He was gone. Kenny commented on the fact that he wished we hadn't stayed there, in the same spot, for so long. A bug was in the process of crawling up the inside of his dungarees. He smacked his leg with his hand. Whatever it was that was inching its way up his leg stopped in its tracks. Kenny raised the pant leg causing the problem and saw a dead spider squished against his bare leg. He made a funny facial expression as he wiped away the deceased spider, which was a combination of red, green, and brown. In order to clean it up he wiped his hand on some dirt nearby. He had a scowl on his face. "Gee, Ben," he said, "what a mess." To make sure the same thing wasn't going to befall me, I kept staring down at my pants, surveying each and every part to check for any slimy bug. Now I'd be thinking about bugs for the rest of the day.

We began to cross through the field leading to the hill. Our chances of encountering the man were very slim. "There's no way we're going to run into that guy," I commented. "Even if we do, we can handle it with no problem, right? Nobody's going to fool with us."

"Yeah, we're a powerful force to reckon with," Kenny bragged. "I'm not worried at all." He strutted about as if he ruled the whole of Folly Hill. Plowing through the tall grass interspersed with bright dandelions was enthralling. The Dandelion Place, Kenny called it.

He'd already dismissed the spider incident as having been an acceptable mishap and returned to his usual cocky mood. It took a lot for my buddy to cringe and give up under pressure. His father, he confided in me, had always pounded into his head that he should always think for himself. Don't buckle, fight the thing that was trying to break your spirit, Kenny reiterated to me. I wondered whether Mr. Annese had succeeded in teaching his son that lesson. Was his father hard on him? I tried like mad to believe this concept but I wasn't really sure nor did I have the gumption to ask him.

Kenny and I took our time as we made our way through the field. It was comprised of tall grass and flowers and weeds. The land was very flat where we were walking; some parts were totally bare, without any growth at all. To our distant right stood countless trees that seemed to signal to us a heavy, more challenging area. That was the section of Folly Hill that reminded me of a vast jungle.

"Why don't we head over there where all those trees are?" I remarked. "I've never been that far into the woods, Kenny. Let's do something different and be brave, okay? I don't care about the man. Who cares about him?" The one thing I didn't want to admit to him was the fact that I was reluctant, even scared, to continue pursuing someone we knew nothing about.

"I care, I want to know who he is," Kenny said firmly. "I want to climb the hill and see what happens." He gave me a cross look.

"You always get your way over me," I asserted, "and I'm sick of it!"

He countered with, "That's tough, buddy." Apparently he was determined to finish what we'd started out to do. And he was steadfast in that conviction. He was downright stubborn, a slow-and-steady type of kid, one who hated anything unfinished.

I shook my head and said, "Okay, but next time we'll do things my way—or else!" He laughed, making me burn inside.

So we slowly climbed the hill. Against my better judgment I went along with his decision. For a moment I thought of myself as the weaker of the two. Why couldn't I simply have turned around and headed home? I always, despite my giving-in nature, possessed a great instinct into most things. In matters that meant the most to me I knew more than others what to do. But the other part of me, the half that didn't want to confront or displease anyone, won out.

We finally were over the hill. Toward our left we saw the man who probably was the same moving figure we'd seen before. He was lying on the grassy slope and seemed to be asleep. A shotgun was by his side. I hit Kenny softly on the shoulder, put a finger to my lips for him to remain quiet, and pointed for us to get out of there fast. I didn't know what he was thinking about, but my friend didn't move. Was he kidding? What was he trying to prove? Whether or not he was didn't matter, because the man heard us and stirred, saw us standing there, and sprung to his feet. He picked up the shotgun and walked our way. He was wearing old brown pants and a red shirt. A black fisherman's cap sat slanted on his head. But the most startling feature about him was his white, yellowish beard. It was long and dirty and gave him a filthy look. I wasn't used to seeing anybody like him. He was old and started jabbering to himself as he approached us. I was so scared I thought Kenny and I were all done for. Was the man angry because we'd interrupted his day? Maybe he was a murderer who'd just escaped from Salem Prison.

"What are you two doing in the middle of the woods?" he asked loudly, keeping hold of his shotgun. Seeing him with his weapon made me fear the worst. Was I going to die right there with Kenny by my side? My parents weren't even there to help me, which made me shutter even more. I wondered what Mom and Dad would think when they found out that I was dead.

"Why aren't you at home with your parents?" the grisly guy said. "If I were you boys, I'd be outside in the sun playing some games. It's not your damn business to be roaming around here in these parts."

I nodded and tried not to appear frightened. Kenny said nothing and stood still. Whenever he was quiet like this, something was wrong. This made me even more alarmed over our predicament.

The man stared at us for what seemed like forever. He looked into our eyes as if he were trying to tell us something. His message was simple and direct. "Get out of here mighty quick, boys," he ordered, "before I lose my patience with you little whippersnappers."

Without looking back once, we both raced down the hill, almost falling in the process, and high-tailed it over the Dandelion Field, through whatever brush we encountered, then passed over the worn path until we reached the stone wall. What a welcomed sight! I couldn't guess how long our scampering toward safety took but I'd bet my life that the two of us broke the world record for that distance. We were gasping for air. And we were crying hysterically. We not only had learned a lesson from this adventure—we were lucky to be alive.

It wasn't until a couple of days later that I saw Kenny. I was standing close to him and yelled, "What a jerk you are! It was your stupid idea in the first place to go looking for that old man. I should punch you right in the mouth. What were you thinking? You don't have a brain in that thick head of yours. That guy could've murdered us, you numbskull, and it would've been your fault. Don't you get it?" Kenny just stood there and said nothing. He did manage to shake his head. With that I turned and hurried toward home.

The Folly Hill story remained a secret between my friend and me for as long as we lived. It bonded us, and became part of our litany of personal legends.

CHAPTER TEN

Even though I loved attending Williams School, a small brick building on the lower end of Elliott Street, there were some hairy moments. I was sick of Miss Callahan and how she criticized some of the students. Other than that, she was an okay teacher. She had been "the stinger" to some of her elementary students. Her favorite "stings" usually came during music appreciation time. Comments such as, "Ben can't sing as well as Joey, anyway, so we'll put Joey up front here," and, "Bobby, please close your music book, as we're about to sing some songs. We don't want him to ruin the class's singing, do we class?" were so cutting and critical that they became legendary in their comic scope. What a comparison between Miss Kent and Miss Callahan. It was the pretty princess versus the big dragon. How ludicrous it was to have put such disparate teachers plying their trade next to one another. They were within hearing distance of one another, no less. I always considered this combination to be hilarious.

I went to Williams School for four years; there were many humorous times. I spent two years in the same room with Miss Kent for the first and second grades; I followed that with two more years with Miss Callahan in an adjoining room for the third and fourth grades. Two rooms, two teachers, four years. Two grades sitting side-by-side and seldom moving. The first grade was on the left side, the second on the right. It was the same setup with the third and fourth grades. If I were to reminisce about it, we were receiving a double dose of education. While we were busy studying lessons as a fourth-grader, we were able to listen in on what the third grade was involved in. We should've all been geniuses. No such thing as a dumb kid should've existed at Williams School. Naturally that wasn't true at all. There were definitely a lot of numbskulls there in the late 40s.

It was a short, enjoyable walk to school and I always looked forward to it with marvelous anticipation. I'd descend the tree-lined hill, Cardinal Road, then take a right on Elliott Street. About a quarter mile down on the left, after always stopping for a few stolen moments to glance at the Maestranzi Farm, where rows of corn and lettuce blended perfectly with the nearby cows and horses and acrid scents surrounding the property, I'd finally come upon Williams School. It was the same wonderful scene every single day: Noisy, but orderly, students would be chatting and yelling among themselves outside the building. They all appeared anxious to begin the day.

A huge glass window dominated the front of the structure and enabled us to peer right into the two classrooms. It was that small! Two tiny spaces serving as coatrooms were on each side of the hallway. After entering one of two doors, the students had to climb a steep stairway on either side of the building to reach the main hall. The first two grades turned left; the third and fourth grades went right. The two teachers stationed in the very center maintained a methodical system whereby each pupil knew how to behave. And somehow, amazingly, it never bothered us kids, the discipline of it all. We expected to be told what to do, and where to proceed, each day.

Sometimes I walked to school alone; other times, I tagged along with Scott or somebody else. My favorite walking mate was Elaine Warner. I was both excited and nervous whenever I saw her coming down Elliott Street, from Lupine Road. I tried to time it perfectly. It was always around seven-thirty. I had nothing against Scott, but he was two years older. After I finished my second year at Williams School, he attended Port School, anyway. I was more apt to hang around kids my own age. The problem was solved automatically as soon as I spotted Elaine.

She was a cute red-haired girl who, like me, was the second child in her family. She was always in a great mood and, I liked to believe, as happy to be around me as I was to be with her. There was a bouncy way about her that picked me up, gave me a surge, an optimistic view of things. I always seemed to do well in school whenever I walked to school with her, especially when she was wearing one of her flowery dresses and a pair of black Mary Jane shoes. She looked super every day! I certainly didn't comprehend the idea of what love was at that age, but I did know how comfortable

I was with Elaine. Was there an ulterior motive involved in my wanting to be with her? Maybe, just maybe, there was. Her older sister, Wanda, who was two years older and shared the same birthday and age as Scott, was the real beauty in East Danvers. I figured that most of the boys had a wild crush on her; she was that pretty. She had long blonde hair and blue eyes, but it was her attitude that was mesmerizing. It was that certain aloofness, that innocent superiority defining her whole being that did it. And she wasn't conceited; she was simply very nice and cordial. Wanda was a lovely and unattainable girl.

Like any kid at Williams School I also suffered some indignities that greatly upset me. They were more than embarrassing; they cut at the very core of my insides. Miss Kent, my first- and second-grade teacher, who sadly became Mrs. Harrison, was involved in the first two of those awful moments in my young life. Why did they have to happen with her? She was one of those once-in-a-lifetime teachers whom all the boys were in love with. She was an adult version of Wanda Warner. Blonde and beautiful, Miss Kent possessed a soft voice that belied her firm nature. Who would've dared misbehave in her class? It was akin to disturbing one of the angels in heaven. Most of the boys were in such awe of her that crossing over into the boundary of bad behavior was out of the question.

The boys' basement in the school was an inner sanctum, a room encased in dreary gray cement and illuminated by one small window. There was one light that, when turned on, helped us see a little bit better. All on its own the place represented to us guys a dark cellar into which we could escape from the world just above it. From there, while I was going to the bathroom I could hear the faint sounds and stirrings of the students in the classrooms just above me. There were two private toilets and three urinals. What a stink they produced. Boys from all four grades constantly asked permission to go. I was positive that both Miss Kent and Miss Callahan, who taught the third and fourth grades, were sick to death of granting an unending stream of students their unalienable right to relieve themselves. (I supposed that the girls' room produced the same effect. Obviously, to my knowledge, none of the guys ever sneaked over to the other side to observe what was going on. We wouldn't have dared to execute such a courageous maneuver! We couldn't have—even if we'd wanted to. We'd have to go all the way down the stairs on the left side, completely separated from the stairs on the right side, which led to the boys' room.)

One of the boys, Richard Bergeron, who was a fledgling actor, would feign having a pain in his stomach by pressing his hands to his midsection. Miss Kent, trying to be as kind as possible in that silly situation, would smile slightly at those clownish antics of Bergeron. As soon as he received permission, Richard would look victoriously around the room to see if anyone was looking and then head downstairs. Miss Kent hadn't been fooled for a second!

Once I didn't make it to the basement on time. I was hesitant in raising my arm and waited far too long for permission to go. It was one of those times when I knew that the mistake I'd made was going to prove irreversibly disastrous. Halfway down the stairs, I ruined my underpants. They were no longer white. A genuine mess was produced! To make matters worse, when I entered the basement bathroom, the light above barely showed me what I was doing.

It was something that took me a long time to get over. It went far beyond anything that could've been possibly rectified. When I was late returning to the classroom upstairs, Miss Kent walked down the stairs and around the corner where she knocked on the cement wall and called, "Ben?" She repeated my name several times.

By then I was crying uncontrollably, unable to respond coherently. I didn't know what to do; I was mortified. How this wonderful woman handled my embarrassing situation shone forever in my mind. It clearly was a perfect example of how a teacher should act in such a situation. As I was cleaning myself up, she waited for me outside the toilet area. "Ben, are you all right?" she asked softly. Her voice was sweet and comforting; I didn't feel threatened by her presence. "Don't worry, do whatever you have to do in there. I understand, okay? Take your time, I'll be right here for you." What seemed like hours but lasted perhaps five or ten minutes, remained a secret between teacher and student. There was a solid connection created there that lasted forever in my heart. But it was the most miserable incident that ever happened to me during my early school years.

Whenever I was sitting in the classroom, I felt totally at ease, secure in my surroundings. Miss Kent was within a few steps of me if I needed anything at all. My mother liked her a lot and, I found out later on, informed the young teacher of a few of my idiosyncrasies. Mom placed great confidence and trust in the fact that someone was always nearby to help me. Was she questioning my ability to fend for myself? I used to sit and stare at Miss Kent. Frankly, I was in awe of the woman. She was both beautiful and nice and I idolized her. I compared her to a fashion model I'd once seen in a magazine. I smiled a lot when I was looking at her. Maybe I just wanted her to realize that I liked her.

One particular afternoon upon my returning home from Williams School my mother suddenly informed me of something that was very disturbing. It concerned Miss Kent who, I was told, was very worried about me. Why in the name of heaven was I always smiling at her in class? She'd phoned Mom and had proceeded to describe my unusual behavior. As this was being related to me, I stood there in front of my mother and began to weep. I didn't believe that Miss Kent felt this way about me. A pin had been stuck into my balloon and temporarily shattered the wonderful image I had of my teacher. The shame I felt was indescribable. Was Miss Kent angry with me? Did she hate me? After all, I looked up to her as a kind of goddess. Why had she phoned my mother? I honestly thought that I no longer would be able to go to school. It was a very serious matter that at first hurt me tremendously.

"Of course not," my mother explained to me, pulling delicately at her hair. She tenderly rubbed my face and looked into my eyes. "Miss Kent isn't angry with you. Don't worry about it."

I was reassured when Mom smiled and poked me in the stomach, causing me to giggle. "Miss Kent likes you, Ben. You're a great kid and a good student. She knows that. It isn't a big deal." I felt much better inside after we'd gone over the situation in detail. There no longer were any misunderstandings about it. "Yes, sweetie, I explained to Miss Kent that you are just a friendly boy who wants everyone to like him. There's nothing to fret about, believe me." After our discussion I was convinced that everything between Miss Kent and me had been cleared up. I had to forget about it. I could go to school as if nothing had happened; everything would be fine.

Then there was the first time I went to Danvers Dance School on Conant Street.

I was sitting with all the boys on one side of the dance floor. The girls were sitting on the opposite side, facing us. A middle-aged, plump woman was at the piano, which was positioned on an elevated stage. The dance instructor, a petite young woman in her late twenties, dressed in a bright red strapless gown and wearing shiny black pumps, was standing in the middle of the floor near the stage equidistant from the girls and the boys. I was very nervous as was evidenced by my constant tugging at my bow tie; it was extremely uncomfortable. The music was going to begin any second. The teacher, Miss June McBride, was stunning and appeared to be very professional. I noticed that the boys, who were between the ages of nine and eleven, were paying strict attention to her. I couldn't stop staring at her dress. I compared her to Miss Kent, whose name had changed to Mrs. Harrison. It was a toss-up as to whom I'd choose between the two. Because I was in the presence of Miss McBride, I chose her. If I were in Miss Kent's class, she'd be my choice. I was, however, still very upset over her marriage. That event changed my attitude toward her considerably; I remembered how crushed I was.

As I gazed over at the substantial audience seated at the rear of the room, I quickly noticed Miss Callahan sitting in the front row, which made me a little uneasy. Those folks, obviously, were either the parents of the participants in the dance class or interested observers who were familiar with them. All the kids sitting in their chairs seemed anxious to start.

Miss Callahan, who wasn't one of my favorite persons of all time, was the future sister-in-law of Miss McBride. After I'd decided to attend that dance class, Miss Callahan told me that my dance instructor was going to marry her youngest brother. That meant Miss McBride was going to become June Callahan. I didn't know why but that bothered me a lot. Miss Callahan certainly looked a lot older than she was. At any rate, I definitely didn't want to make a spectacle of myself that evening in front of my fourth-grade teacher.

The music began; the plump woman playing the piano did a good job. As expected, it was a foxtrot. Prior to each dance Miss McBride demonstrated to us the correct steps. The foxtrot was simple: "One, two, step together; one, two, step together." I clumsily walked across the floor and, as the boys were instructed to do, chose a girl to be my dancing partner. It wasn't as if every guy raced across the floor to the other side in frantic pursuit of his eventual choice. If anything, each boy was deliberate in deciding the girl he wanted to dance with.

I bowed in front of a girl. All of the boys bowed almost at the same instant. It was as if you were winding up many dolls at once and the dolls began to move on cue as you put them down.

I followed the girl I'd chosen to the center of the dance floor. She was at least three inches taller than I was. We looked like Mutt and Jeff, but she was very cute. Her name, she whispered to me, was Jane. She was wearing a yellow dress and I liked her smile a lot. The next thing that happened to me on the dance floor was extremely embarrassing. Right after I took her right hand and put it in my left hand, I moved my right arm around her but my right hand fell by accident on her bum. I was mortified for a moment, yet I was able to recover by quickly raising my arm and placing my hand on the bottom of her back. Thank God, she didn't say a word about it. I really couldn't help what I'd done. She was so tall that I misjudged my grasp. As we danced around the floor to the music I felt great. I considered myself an excellent dancer as my confidence soared.

The partner I'd picked would be with me for about six dances. That was a good thing. After that I had to choose another girl, which I didn't relish. The second time around I might not be so lucky. I barely was able to focus on one girl at a time. I didn't want to get too confused. My grandfather always joked with me by saying that no boy was capable of figuring girls out; they were far too complicated. I didn't know what he meant by that at the time, but I kept his advice in the back of my mind. He surely knew something about girls, though. He'd been married forever to one. Either he was doing something right or my grandmother simply didn't realize what was going on over there in Salem.

My dances with Jane were wonderful; being next to her on the dance floor gave me goose bumps. It was the first time in my life when being so close to a girl produced such a marvelous feeling. Even though I had walked to school with Elaine Warner many times, we never had so much as touched. I not only liked the way Jane conducted herself on the dance floor but I also loved the perfume she had on. It smelled like lilacs. There was no doubt in my mind that we were the best couple there. No other pair danced as well as the two of us. If I weren't careful all the girls in the class would want to dance with me. My mother, who was a great pianist, taught me many steps. She played the piano in the living room while I practiced the moves with an imaginary partner. She told me many times that I should be a professional dancer. If any kid at Williams School ever found out that I practiced with my mother, I'd be laughed out of the school. "Oh, guess what guys, Ben's doing those sissy dances at home with his Mom." The verbal jabs at me would've never ceased. So I had to be careful not to tell a soul about it. It was always smarter to keep things to myself.

My mother had always pushed dancing and singing my way. To think that she was an accomplished concert pianist and none of her sons had ever learned anything about the piano was a disgrace. I wondered whose fault it was that sports came first.

As that evening of dancing faded into a soothing memory, I always cherished my first dance with Jane, especially my misplaced hand. It was surely an awkward moment. I did dance with other girls, too. It'd been a totally positive few hours. It was the first time I'd ever done anything like that and I loved every minute of it. It was because my mother had suggested it to me in the first place. I anticipated many more evenings like that one.

CHAPTER ELEVEN

I was sitting in the waiting room of Jeffers Funeral Home. My mind seemed to be nowhere and everywhere all at once. It was as if I were floating around in the thin air occupying the space around me. It was suffocating me and I felt numb. My hands had lost their sensation because I'd never experienced such a loss as this. All my emotions were coming together. Before this happened, I always had been able to control myself reasonably well. I became muddled over this. I gazed toward the main room across the hall and saw my father's body lying in a casket, a dark brown color. Countless flowers that produced a brilliant rainbow were arranged all around him. I went over slowly to the casket and stood there silently, afraid and a little dizzy. My father, his face a pasty white and his hands folded exposing his Masonic ring, was wearing a navy blue suit. He was so still that I didn't believe what I was seeing. I felt sick over it. He'd controlled me for thirty-five years and, for some reason, I felt cheated. I knew he loved me but I also believed he despised me. I'd done nothing without his firm approval. If he disapproved of anything I was doing, I stopped doing it. Everything with him was either in the affirmative or in the negative. There was nothing in the middle. It didn't matter whether it concerned my friends, my dates, or my jobs. He had something to say about it. Whatever I did or said that was considered wrong by him carried with it a consequence. I didn't know why, but I was the one who always felt guilty about how he treated me. While I was doing all those countless things for him at home, Scott and Andy grew up in a normal way, went to college, got good jobs and got married in one big swoop. I remained at home, going absolutely nowhere. Even when I had that steady girlfriend, Janice, he without fail made me go to the store for peanut butter and ice cream just as I was about to head out the door on a date, ruining my good time. That didn't matter to him. He knew that I was in a hurry and still proceeded to get in the way of my happiness. He knew exactly what he was doing. Whenever I seemed to be picking myself up, he knocked me down again. Yet I was the one who felt badly about it.

On the other hand, Mr. Scott Robblee was sometimes exceedingly kind to me. It varied, according to the circumstance. There were many things that my father and I did together. We went to those Boston Celtic championship games at the old Boston Garden in the glory days of Bob Cousy and Bill Russell. We ate those expensive meals in Tampa, Florida, at the Careless Navigator Restaurant when he had me flown down south for spring practice to be alone with him. He attended my baseball and football games in order to witness and judge his second son's performance, expecting me to excel above and beyond my actual ability. He met those dates of mine beforehand to see if the girls were up to his specifications.

He examined my report card to make sure I was meeting his expectations, especially in math, my poorest subject. They were all the highs and lows that existed between my father and me. It was all over!

The panic that gripped me was intolerable. Even though I knew distinctly that he had been very ill with cancer, I wasn't ready for his death. I both relied on and feared my father. As much as I wanted to be near him, I also wished to flee from him. It was a tug-of-war that he always won. Did I do my part to meet him halfway? Several times I'd approached Dad with the intent of explaining how I felt about things, but it simply didn't work. I felt relieved standing before the casket, no longer having to answer to him. But with this abrupt loss of weight from my shoulders, I also found it impossible to rid myself of my intense guilt. I wasn't sure how to handle it. The only person who fully comprehended my state of mind was my mother, Grace Foster Robblee, a wonder of a woman. She was someone who had stuck by me. I realized my life hadn't mirrored, in any way, my two brothers' lives. Even though I believed Mom didn't have the same respect for me that she had for her two other sons, at least she never judged me openly. She loved me as much as she loved them. My father, however, was open in his disapproval of me. But as I gazed down at him, it mattered no more.

Whereas Scott and Andy were married and well employed, I was unmarried and had jumped around many insignificant jobs. That was ultimately what people looked at. They didn't understand that I was, more or less, forced into staying at home following my untimely injury, after which I was never the same person. But many people who knew me swore that no one had made me remain with my parents. Maybe that was true but there were a lot of subtle things they didn't see. I decided in my mind to let the issue rest there. I couldn't spend the rest of my life explaining things to them.

I had to turn my situation around even though there was a terrible foundation to build on. From the very beginning it hadn't gone right for me. My therapist told me that once the snowballing had begun, there was no stopping it. Only I could accomplish that; it was up to me. There had to be a readjustment process.

After viewing Dad in the main room, I went back and sat down on the large sofa. "Come here," my mother said, waving at me from the hallway. I quickly got up and went over to her. There were two women standing next to her. "I want you to meet Thelma Goodale, Ben. Thelma was my roommate at Westbrook Junior College. Do you believe it? And this is Wilma Sudbury, the woman responsible for my becoming interested in the piano many years ago." It was obvious that Mom had been crying but somehow she appeared at ease with these two ladies. The Goodale woman, who had a pretty face and was considerably overweight, wore a black dress that was quite becoming on her. Wilma, who was much older than my mother, was nonetheless a stunning lady who I figured was once very beautiful. Instantly I was attracted to her. I imagined myself being with her when she was a young woman, the two of us going to a concert all dressed up. "Ben has been wonderful to me," Mom related. "I can't tell you ladies how much he has meant to me these last few years." She kissed me tenderly on the cheek, her eyes welling up in the process. "Someday Ben is going to meet a lovely girl, right Ben?" she said, touching my shoulder.

I didn't believe the things that came into my mind in the midst of such an emotional avalanche. Without my father I felt lost and uncomfortable. He was no longer alive to help or hinder me. There were no more excuses. Dr. Amanda Grossman, my therapist, a woman in her fifties, had loads of faith in me. She emphasized that a new life awaited me, as if I were beginning a new diet. She was unlike most analysts; she didn't baby me and agree with whatever I spilled out. She even intimated to me, in a shocking way, how she herself overcame her own hatred and distrust of men. "I never chose my partners wisely, Ben," she maintained, crossing her long legs as she sat in the corner of the room. Her form of therapy was working for me. I had been going to see her at the hospital for several months.

To sit or stand in a funeral home for four hours was torturous: two hours in the afternoon and two more hours in the evening was a grinding process. That was the usual time frame for people to come together in order to observe and honor a deceased person. On that night there was a considerable crowd, for which I was thankful. I was trying to force myself to go over and speak with my friends and acquaintances; it was the least I could do. My mother further introduced me to several individuals that I'd never met. It was frantic—but

I had to do it. I certainly was forced by the situation to put on a positive face, one that appeared as if I weren't falling apart.

Every so often I walked down the beautifully carpeted hall and checked the guest register. I was nosy. I wanted to know who had come to see my father. This might boost my spirits, enabling me to continue more easily. I was appreciative to those considerate mourners who had taken the time to acknowledge my father's life. They didn't have to attend but they did. I looked over toward the casket and saw Scott engaged in what seemed to be an emotional discussion with three guys. All four were laughing and shaking their heads in unison. What was going on? I stared at them, wondering. They probably were talking about Dad. It was perhaps something that brought back fond memories. I decided to find out who they were. I wasn't able to place them, but the faces of those three men looked familiar. I'd seen them somewhere. I racked my brain and tried to remember. It didn't ring a bell. How could I expect myself to remember or recognize anyone at such a sad moment? I wasn't able to focus on anything. My mind was clouded by confusion. It was a miracle that I was still standing; my only goal was to survive the ordeal.

Scott introduced me to the Sorensen brothers, Walter and Sam, and "Veal" Capozzi, all from Salem. It suddenly came to me! They were three of the fellows who had played for the old Salem Witches. They used to be the grubby and rude-talking kids who lived near my father's welding shop. Thanks to my father, they played ball right beside the railroad tracks in Salem. I didn't believe what was happening. How was it that after twenty-five years they were there? They stood in front of the very man who had reversed their fortunes. His death brought adversaries on the field of play together to celebrate a man's caring ways. "Your father was a mentor to us," Walter said proudly as he shook my hand. "I don't know what would've happened to me if I hadn't known him." His eyes were misty as he spoke. Walter seemed sincere, was eager to reveal to two sons what their father had meant to him and several other hooligans. Yes, they had been juvenile delinquents who on many occasions had vandalized my father's welding shop. They even went so far as to smash through the door lock. Their parents, or lack of them, weren't present to discipline them. They were intimidating and tough customers. While attending the old Phillips School off Salem Common, they challenged every rule ever devised by the authorities. They were suspended, expelled, or punished unmercifully. It didn't solve anything. That was, until one night very late, while they were snooping around inside the shop, generally just acting like crooks, my Dad accompanied by George, his huge specimen of a foreman who resembled a wrestler, suddenly showed up. Walter grinned when he related to me the emotional impact visited upon the young criminals when they encountered head-on those two furious men. Walter raised his arms in jest. Then he covered his eyes with his hands. What could the hapless boys do? They stood there, frozen in fear, in the dark shop. They didn't have a prayer. They surely weren't having fun anymore. The two shadowy figures remained motionless in the doorway and stared them down. There was no place for them to run to, no escape route. The four kids broke down in tears. "I think it was one of the few times I ever cried in front of someone," Walter admitted. "It was the first occasion when I actually felt not only defeated but also miserable over what I'd done. Everything came together, as in the matching pieces of a puzzle."

My father demanded that the boys report to his shop after school the following afternoon. He was aided by the presence of his enormous henchman. If they didn't do as they were told, he'd take steps that were severe. Did they get the point? Walter, Sam, Veal, and the fourth kid, no longer alive, understood clearly.

They did exactly as they were told. The four guys appeared right after school the next day. The instructions my Dad gave them were simple enough. There was a trade involved, however, in the deal. They had to atone for their wrongdoing by working in the shop a couple of hours a day until he was satisfied with their performance. They had to clean up and do odd jobs that Dad's workmen didn't have the time to do. They even had to put away the men's tools if they were told to. This wasn't just a punishment, my father impressed upon them. No, it was also a lesson. The problem with them was that they never had learned correct manners. The owner of the welding shop told them he also had committed many blunders in his time. The Salem kids listened intently to my father. Yes, as a defiant youngster growing up in Salem, he'd been a downright brat at times. Being an only child, he struggled in his relationships with his peers. Though he wanted to stand out in the crowd, he often didn't succeed in that department. And when he didn't succeed, he struck out in revenge. He beat up a couple of bullies on the grounds of Horace Mann School as an eighth-grader, paying dearly for that incident. At Salem High School, because Dad wasn't on the first team in basketball, he quit the squad by throwing his uniform at the coach. Those antics didn't go down in the annuals of Salem High Sports as being particularly praiseworthy. But, my father admitted to the boys, he'd learned from his actions and decided to travel an easier, more sensible path. In fact, after college, he came back and visited his old coach. Not only that, he apologized to him. In the following years they became close friends.

Walter Sorensen, most of all, wanted us to understand the main reason he was present at my father's wake. He felt he had to pay homage to my Dad, to the only person who ever took him under his wing and directed him toward a worthwhile life. Walter wondered what would've happened to him hadn't he been caught red-handed that night in the shop. It was a blessing. He eventually finished high school, graduated from Boston University and landed a job with the government.

As Walter told me this, a chill came over me. It was one of the strangest sensations I'd ever had, almost like an electric shock. Here was a man standing in front of my father's casket and speaking honestly and directly to my brother Scott and me about him. He valued having met my father and having gone through the harrowing experiences that straightened out his life.

I was conflicted in my thoughts. It was as if I were dodging pellets as they came zooming at my head. I reflected on what I'd just heard, but in the process of trying to absorb it, I felt agitated. Here was a guy who had nothing bad to say about my father. I couldn't deal with that. I often questioned whether my father knew how much power he wielded over me. I was fairly sure he did. He had to realize that every time he stomped on me, it wasn't for my benefit. After I got badly hurt in football my senior year, rendering me almost useless for a decade and hopelessly at the mercy of my parents, especially my mother, things were never the same. Mom plainly understood this. Had Dad?

Four hours in the funeral home seemed like four days. I remembered two high school athletes, teammates of mine, who had died tragically at a young age. One of them, Donny, was a close friend who committed suicide by hanging himself at the age of thirty. The other one, Robert, was a mere nineteen. He was accidentally shot to death in his college dorm room during a prank. The two were opposites in every respect. Donny never really had a chance in life—Robert did. Their early deaths often made me meditate on the sanctity of life, especially when I went to a wake or funeral.

There were thirty minutes to go. Most of the visitors, including Veal and the Sorensen men had left, making it much more peaceful. My mother was in a waiting room talking with a dear friend of my father. The man was extremely upset over Dad's death. He'd been there for at least an hour; I'd noticed him immediately upon his entering Jeffers Funeral Home. On several occasions I was invited by Dad to join them for lunch. Mr. Kelly worked for Sylvania, a company my father did business with. That's how they'd met many years ago. They were very close. I'd dropped by the shop at the convenient hour of noon, causing Dad to burst out laughing. I wasn't fooling him for a second. Yes, I was hungry. And I also was confident that I'd be treated once again to a super meal at one of Salem's fine restaurants.

A free meal, fifty free meals, never assuaged the self-reproach I felt because I didn't have a job. My father worked hard, as did Mr. Kelly.

I left the funeral home that night with my mother and realized I had to do something from that point on to change my life, even though I was frightened and uncertain what that might be.

CHAPTER TWELVE

By 1951 the East Danvers Red Sox had disbanded. Sadly, Joey Buccella had moved to New Mexico after his father had gotten an important job there. I heard he was in the mattress business. I received a couple of letters from Joey. More than half the words were spelled incorrectly. In his case, I saw that Miss Kent and Miss Callahan had both been unsuccessful in their futile attempts to teach him anything. Joey's strong attraction to girls and their reciprocal feelings probably had been his downfall in school. Even though he was so good-looking, apparently he thought he didn't have to know how to spell. "We don get no sno her in New Mexico," he wrote. I never showed his letters to my mother. She would've been mortified by them. "He's such a nice-looking boy, too," she would've said, as if looks had anything to do with it. "What a shame."

I stopped seeing Kenny Annese so much. I knew this was inevitable. Being two years younger than I was, Kenny remained at Williams School. I went over to Port School. This meant a big adjustment for me. The distance was far greater and there were many more kids to contend with. And there were more girls. No longer could I depend on

Miss Kent's assistance and understanding. As for Miss Callahan's third- and fourth-grade classes, I never missed them at all.

My grandparents' large, three-storied house was located in North Salem. They'd been Salem residents for over fifty years, ever since moving from the rambling, quiet hills of New Hampshire just before the beginning of the 1900s. My grandmother emphasized that they were certified Yankees, through and through. She was a proud, stubborn woman who stressed that she was traced way back to the Mayflower crowd. My Grandma and Grandpa Foster were simple, honest, hard-working people. She always gave me the impression that there had been very few complications and problems in their young lives that they hadn't been able to tend to in the proper manner. The end of the 1800s hadn't been an easy time; they hadn't had the conveniences of modern times. Whenever I visited them, which was often, it stirred up within me a feeling of such excitement that I could barely wait for my father to drive me to their place.

They were full of stories detailing the countless happenings of the previous century. There had been some hair-raising incidents that had rattled the seemingly innocent community of Wolfeboro.

My mother's mother, Edith Tibbetts Foster, we called "Nanny." When she was conceived, the Lord had found it in His kind power to create an exceptional human being. When I was a naïve youngster, I didn't believe that she possessed a single flaw. Perhaps she was decidedly narrow-minded, but that depended on a person's point of view. That trait was easily attributed to the fact that she'd not been exposed to the questionably raw behavior of people from the outside. Her town had been removed from the confusion of the rest of the world. Having come from what she claimed was a pure dot on the New England map, specifically the state that had the majestic White Mountains and the clean air to go along with it, she'd been fed the unalterable niceties of her era. A healthy mixture of morality and sternness had been responsible for the spreading out of much goodness around the area.

"If only," Nanny said, touching her soft white hair that was piled high on her head and somehow held together by some contraption in the back, "everyone had been brought up with the same principles that I had, the world would've never had any wars."

"Bampy" was cut from a different cloth. Percy E. Foster was my favorite person of all time! Since I'd been a toddler I'd hung around him as if my very life depended on it. Maybe it did. Never in the twenty-eight years that we shared the universe did he ever utter a mean word or bawl me out for an indiscretion. Whereas he was my mother's Dad, I found it to be of no small coincidence that he had the distinction with his only daughter of being included on my most-loved-people-in-the-world list. After the two of them, I could honestly say there was no one else that I respected as much.

There were many unforgettable things that Bampy and I did together when I visited their place on Oakland Street. I considered those times with him as being not merely special but also instructive. We understood each other perfectly. Even in Nanny's presence, we transcended her thoughts and actions and focused on each other. There was no way she knew what was going on, or so I thought. This didn't mean that we ignored her. On the contrary, she was included in most of our activities. When we got out the cards to play canasta, the three of us, seated at the kitchen table, fought it out for supremacy. The seating arrangement was no accident. It was such that I served Bampy my chosen card. He in turn served his card to my grandmother. And she concluded the cycle by serving me a card. Whereas I was cautious not to give him any card too good, he was dead set not to ever let Nanny have a decent card. Her winning the game would've ruined his day. He wouldn't have slept well. The final tally, after a period of several years, ended up with my winning twenty-six games, Nanny's winning sixteen and Bampy's triumphing only ten times. To save those contests for posterity, I meticulously kept the score of each one by writing them down on notebook paper that I'd bought from a Woolworth Store in Danvers. Each game had the exact date and time we'd played with other important things also mentioned, such as the weather and the meal of the day. I was always glad that I kept those valuable records in a safe place.

I came downstairs at eight in the morning and saw my grandmother in the pantry, which adjoined the spacious kitchen. I'd slept like an angel—maybe because I really was in Heaven. I never forgot the fresh smell of the sheets. My grandmother always kept such a clean house. I even enjoyed taking a bath each evening I spent there. It was better than being in an expensive hotel. She always had Camay on hand, my favorite soap.

Bampy had bought that beautiful gray structure half-way up a hill at the incredibly low price of three thousand dollars. My grandparents were newlyweds looking for a nice location on the North Shore. With its history Salem was a perfect spot to begin their new life together. They also had considered living in the city of Lynn. In those days there was no such thing as a transportation problem. Everything was simple and safe. People's lives weren't cluttered.

Peeking around the corner of the kitchen into the pantry, I saw my grandmother working hard. She always was busy doing something around the house. Cleaning, cooking, and washing were but a few of the things to do on her daily agenda. Hard work was her sustenance and it never ceased. But she considered her number one job to be the caring of her husband. Pleasing him was her main priority. I found out much later, after they were both gone, that she'd once intimated to my Aunt Helen, her daughter-in-law, how her constant devotion to "good old Percy" had been her major mistake in life. It had robbed her of many things. Oh sure, she loved him, yet she also was imprisoned by an unending obligation. There was never any doubt about that. Never had he gone without a meal or an ironed shirt in their long marriage. How could any woman, she'd angrily asked my Aunt Helen, accomplish any personal goals if she were occupied one hundred percent of the time with her family? It was easy to see a parallel there with my mother's marital plight. In much the same manner Grace Foster Robblee, my Mom, had followed precisely the same path as Edith Tibbetts Foster. Devotion to marriage and deep love were welded together to produce a successful, though unequal, union. In both cases there was a fully contented man and a tolerant woman who thought she was happy because she was well taken care of by her husband—yet she was still unfulfilled. Aunt Helen, the unofficial historian of the family tree, told me that the two women probably didn't know any better or, if they did, fully accepted their plight.

Nanny was mixing pancake batter in the pantry. It was her best breakfast, along with bacon and sausages and orange juice. Whenever I ate over there, for some reason the food tasted a lot better. My mother was a good cook but I preferred my grandmother's cooking any day of the week. I didn't have to share the food with Scott and Andy. I felt as if my grandmother always paid special attention to me. Even though I never asked Scott if he received the same attention from her, I was hoping he didn't. I was sharing something all by myself. Plus no one else in my family was there to spoil my fun. I knew that I shouldn't have those awful thoughts. They ran counter to everything my parents had taught me.

But when I spent this time with Nanny and Bampy I was totally on my own. I expressed myself much more freely. Bampy was objective when it came to my shaky relationship with my father. Understandably he loved and respected my Dad for several reasons. Scott Sr. was married to his only daughter following a prolonged battle among several suitors for Grace's hand. Grace Foster was very popular at Salem High with the boys and was extremely smart and pretty in a petite kind of way. She won the "Miss Pequot Mills" contest at the age of seventeen. After high school she attended and graduated from Westbrook Junior College in Maine, where she majored in music and subsequently became a classical pianist. There were no artistic boundaries she didn't cross. She was adept in sculpting, painting, and writing poetry. She conquered everything she attempted "gracefully," as Aunt Helen often joked.

The main reason for Bampy's fondness toward his son-in-law centered on a deal they'd made before my parents' wedding. It seemed that Dad didn't get along with his father, Gaylord Robblee, who was a local blacksmith in Salem. The conflict arose when Grandpa Robblee whom I met only a couple of times in my life insisted that his son also become a blacksmith. Gaylord said it was the only thing to do because he was the only blacksmith in the whole surrounding area, covering many miles. He figured Scott also would do splendidly in that business. Gaylord refused to take no for an answer. But my father, being a single-minded young man, wanted to start his own welding business after college.

There was, however, one huge problem that stood in his way: money. So he did what any aspiring son trying to impress his father would do. Scott explained his plan to his Dad and, in the bargain, asked him for a loan of several hundred dollars. He was determined to go through with his dream. Gaylord balked. He figured Scott's plan was an affront to his authority. The stubborn father refused the equally-as-stubborn son. A battle of wills ensued that lasted a lifetime. It turned into a feud that every member of the involved families whispered about.

After much thought, the future groom decided to ask his soon-to-be father-in-law for the money. He had nothing to lose, he reasoned. With his arms outstretched, Percy E. Foster welcomed the opportunity to help him. The groundwork had been set. Armed with the capital to begin his new enterprise, my father took his big gamble in life and opened a welding shop.

Not only was Dad a talented welder but he also did the labor of two men. At first he was the company's only employee. Long days and nights working at projects he pounded the pavement to find resulted in his positive launching of the business. Over a period of a few years as his family grew, his determination at work paid off. He was a driven man who also possessed the smarts to succeed. His crew at the shop, with a base of four crackerjack welders and a handful of helpers, reaped enormous benefits for him. The late 30s into the early 40s were tough times economically, but the underlying prospect for growth was there. With some clever juggling of his men, matching the right welders to the right jobs, my father developed a vastly successful company. His three sons and wife never knew the inner workings of his business. It was only later on that I learned from his friends that he'd been an outstanding businessman. All the big-business names on the North Shore and Boston hired the Scott Robblee Welding Company to do jobs for them. Even some wealthy families who owned estates in Beverly Farms used him for some lucrative assignments. The surrounding town governments had a need for him to complete numerous undertakings, which he gladly took on. Everything came into place for him. My father always loved the old guy who'd paved the way for him.

On the opposite pole, his undying resentment toward his father never wavered. It was a hatred that was such a waste. It was something that carried with it dire consequences. My brothers and I rarely saw our other set of grandparents.

I knew that Bampy and my father were close. Even though Bampy loved me dearly and I loved him, there was a delicate balancing act involved as far as what I could admit to him. I was positive he realized there was a rift between my father and me. He'd have to be a moron not to see it. But he probably didn't put much stock in its seriousness. When my father picked me up from Bampy's house to head home, there was nothing overtly hostile demonstrated between us in front of Bampy. However, it made me feel awkward. How did my grandfather really know anything potentially explosive existed? He never heard anything negative about my father and me from Nanny who was very tight-lipped. She only told him what he wanted to hear. Or what she considered it was safe for her to divulge to her husband.

I always got a genuine kick out of the shenanigans between Nanny and Bampy. It was like listening to a Burns-and-Allen Comedy Show. He was the most deliberate man on the planet. Slow to most people meant fast to him. He took forever getting ready in the bathroom before coming to the kitchen table to eat. She yelled her brains out for him to, "Hurry it up, will you? Your food is getting cold, Pa. For goodness sake." She rolled her eyes at me.

And here I was, sitting impatiently, half starving to death as I waited for the old codger to appear. I was laughing under my breath. Finally he exited the bathroom, puttering away all the while, before sitting down for supper. The world waited for the old man.

Clearing his throat, he said in a most irritating way, "Is everything ready, Edith?" After looking at the scrumptious spread before him, seeing that everything was okay, he winked at me and concluded with, "Good, are we ready to eat, Ben?" At that point the three of us were ravenous and began to eat.

CHAPTER THIRTEEN

All during my formative years my Aunt Helen was the one in the family who knew everything about everyone and wasn't shy about imparting any information to me. As I progressively became the hearing vessel for all the family gossip she told me, I learned more about the reasons for my father's attitude toward me, or I thought I did. Early on my aunt was always eager to help out her favorite nephew by spilling the beans, loading me with extremely useful information. But, unfortunately, it was a shame I didn't pay much attention to her. If I had, perhaps I could've used this as ammunition to better confront my issues with Dad.

The famous Dr. Tucker Story was passed around for years in the Robblee and Foster families. And with time it developed in its own dramatic way.

At the tender age of six months, as both Grandma Foster and Aunt Helen related it, reassuring everyone of its accuracy, I developed a critical case of pneumonia. Extremely upset over my illness, my mother needed medication to settle her down. When she almost went over the edge, Nanny naturally became very concerned over her daughter. She called upon her trusted physician, Dr. Tucker, who showed up that evening at our house. Apparently it was touch-and-go for me for a couple of days. Dr. Tucker, my aunt verified, was one of those rare old doctors whose methods of treatment bordered on the line between acceptability and experimental. He informed Mom the situation was desperate but said I could lick it. Any means would suffice. What he decided to do with me could be termed by most folks as bizarre, way beyond the medical realm of reason, especially when treating a baby. My getting better depended on bringing my high fever down. My grandmother, who was a moral person above all else, was dead set against what Dr. Tucker suggested. How on earth, she asked him, did he even consider such a nitwit thing? Even if it saved my life, Nanny asserted, what he wanted to do was wrong, immoral. My aunt, who was my mother's chum and confidante, convinced Mom it was worth a try.

Anything that could save Benjamin Robblee was fine with both Aunt Helen and my mother. "Let's get going, Dr. Tucker," Mom said, looking seriously at him. Phooey with principle. Everyone but Nanny was convinced; my father apparently remained silent.

My temperature remained high for the first hour after Dr. Tucker had poured a small amount of whiskey down my throat. It was difficult for him to do this; I had to be propped up so that I wouldn't choke to death. But slowly over the next couple of hours my temperature dropped to about one hundred degrees. "I think Ben is going to make it just fine, Mrs. Robblee," the doctor whispered. During the fourth hour he slowly administered another small amount of whisky. After being given those two doses of the immoral stuff, I began to get better. Within several more hours my temperature was normal, which meant I was going to recover.

All was wonderful with the world. It was a miracle that I survived the ordeal. There was general rejoicing in the Robblee and Foster households. My mother, Aunt Helen, and her husband, my Uncle Bennie, were speechless. My mother cried. Nanny and Bampy, my future card partners, were ecstatic. Nanny gave the credit to God, not the whiskey. My father, as Aunt Helen told me years later, was so stunned that he displayed no emotion whatsoever.

There were conflicting interpretations concerning my dangerous brush with pneumonia. My mother explained to me long after my father's death, when some of my bitterness and misunderstanding had gone by the wayside, that my Aunt Helen was never particularly fond of Dad and, in fact, resented the fact that she was never able to have a child. "You must understand, Ben, that it wasn't your aunt's fault for thinking the way she did," my mother declared. "People are the way they are for a good reason." Mom was very sick and dying at the time of that discussion. "Don't judge your father by what other people say about him, remember that." Why hadn't my mother related that to me when I was much younger and could've benefited from it?

CHAPTER FOURTEEN

My actual period of maturing began upon my entering Port School. I was more cognizant of certain things that never before had even concerned me. I discovered that danger was always present, watching for its chance to pounce upon the first vulnerable soul it saw. Up until I was ten, throughout my Williams School years, I'd been residing within a certain circumference of safety.

The first thing that happened to me at Port School wasn't classified as a positive experience. I was older and yet wasn't prepared for any drastic changes in my school life.

On my first day at Port school, within only five minutes, I met a kid whose name was Charlie. It was as if someone had bumped into me by mistake and I was to blame. This was my introduction to Port School. Just like that I was in a certain amount of trouble. I was facing a confrontation before class had begun. I didn't even know who my fifth-grade teacher was; I hadn't entered the building yet.

"Hey, you," this tough guy said. "Who are you?" He stood there with two other fellows, preventing me from passing. The boy who had spoken had a round, fat face, blond hair, and was wearing a black leather jacket. Another guy, just in back of him, was real skinny and his black, greasy hair matched his leather jacket perfectly. The third guy didn't seem to belong with the other two: he was clean-cut with short brown hair and wore a simple green jacket. I didn't understand what the blond kid was trying to prove by acting so tough. I'd never encountered such a threat in my life.

"Me? I'm Ben Robblee," I answered, trembling.

"Yeah? I'm Charlie. Remember this, Ben Robblee, you don't own this school." Then the three of them walked away. I stood there, startled, not knowing what to do. And so I just went to my classroom.

My fifth-grade teacher was named Miss Potter. She was older than Miss Callahan, my fourth-grade teacher at Williams School. The one thing I noticed about her was her chin. It was very fat and the skin just hung there. The front of Miss Potter's neck looked like a chicken's. It reminded me immediately of Joey Buccella's grandmother and her butchering in the summer. Miss Potter also wore weird round glasses. Other than that she seemed nice enough. I ascertained right away that she was a strict teacher just by the solemn sound of her voice. She looked around the room, studying each pupil to see if she had any bad apples to deal with. She seemed satisfied that she had none. I was seated in the front seat of the middle row, directly in front of her desk, not my favorite seating arrangement. I much preferred to sit in the back corner of a classroom. It was safer and it gave me more room to breathe. I was able to think more clearly there, with a great view of the goings-on. I felt, sitting up front, that everyone, especially the teacher, witnessed every single move I made. All eyes were on her and they were on me, too.

Sitting beside me to my left was a skinny kid whose name was Eddie Howard. I figured out right away that he was a real cut-up, the future class clown. He reminded me of "Jughead" in the "Archie" comics. He began our relationship by making faces when Miss Potter wasn't looking. That was smart, I thought. Then he turned to me to confirm whether or not I was paying any attention to him. I was. I didn't laugh, but I smiled. He was a real Red Skelton in the making. His light brown hair was close-cropped and he had two large front teeth that, for some odd reason, went perfectly with the oval shape of his face. He kept whispering something unintelligible to me, believing all the while that I heard him. I kept smiling, as if I did. For the entire morning this ridiculous exchange between us continued. It was starting to get to me.

At noontime Miss Potter called for the two of us to come up to the front desk. I knew it. She wasn't stupid, after all. She was the teacher and we were two foolish kids. She took us aside and spoke to both of us about our behavior. Unbelievably she'd witnessed everything. "Stop making those funny faces," she ordered, pointing at Eddie. "And stop bothering your neighbor with your chitchat. Do you understand?" Her chin waggled as she talked; I dreaded Eddie's reaction to all this. Was he going to say or do something stupid and get us into more trouble? A few seconds later Eddie, seeming shell-shocked, answered, "Yes, Miss Potter." Instantly I was relieved.

She wasn't through with us. Then she looked sternly at me. Her tone lessened in its intensity but I knew by the look on her face that she was serious. "Stop encouraging your friend," she emphasized. She didn't stop staring me down until I nodded my head, agreeing with her. We then were allowed to return to our desks for lunch.

I often took a bus to Port School because my father usually left for work way before its arrival. This made me happy. I waited for Danny Doheney, then the two of us stood at the juncture of Cardinal Road and Elliott Street to catch a ride. Within a short time a noisy bus coming from North Beverly pulled up, emitting its obscene fumes before coming to a complete stop. I liked the smell of the smoke, a combination of rotten eggs and some disgusting chemical. It gave me satisfaction that I was going to school without the help of my father. I much preferred to be with Danny or even by myself. I just didn't feel comfortable when I was sitting next to my father in the front seat of his white Continental. I knew it wasn't true but I had it stuck in the back of my mind that he didn't really enjoy taking me along with him, that he wanted to give me the dime to go by bus.

Danny and I stepped onto the bus. It was a cool, invigorating autumn day and the multi-colored leaves were flying all over the place. This wasn't a school bus. We didn't have any special vehicles that took us back and forth. The orange vehicle carried all the people from the Beverly and Danvers area who were going to their various jobs. A few kids always caught a ride.

What I was looking forward to the most, however, was whether or not the woman with the platinum blonde hair would be sitting in the second row in front next to the window. That excited me and made my day complete. Four out of five days she was there. As I passed her on this crisp morning, I got a tremendous whiff of her perfume. It was the most powerful, tantalizing smell I'd ever sniffed, making me feel momentarily disoriented. For that moment I was being forced into a forbidden fantasy, something soothing and irresistible.

Another inaccessible feature to this beautiful woman, whose age I couldn't begin to guess, was the abundant amount of bright red lipstick she was wearing. It looked like wet strawberry spread out evenly over her lips. They were the greatest lips I'd ever seen. I felt a bit bewildered thinking about it but I wondered what it must've felt like for a man to kiss her. Was she married? What joy it must've been for her husband. He'd be totally smeared by the red stuff. But the sensation had to be most gratifying. I honestly believed that this gorgeous woman introduced me to a new universe. Hopefully there were more women like her residing somewhere out there. Who would ever want to escape their clutches? Not me.

As always, Danny and I sat down in the row right

behind the woman. I looked at him and he was peering at a baseball magazine he'd brought along; everything in his life concerned sports, anyway. I said nothing to Danny about my secret fascination with the blonde. There was no way he'd read anything into the fact that I always chose to sit in the exact same seat every time. He was unaware of such things.

Within several weeks of attending Port School, I started to fit in with the rest of the kids. The Wednesday after Labor Day when I'd had words with that boy, I'd been the new guy on the scene. Now things were far different. There was no need to fret over that incident. The fourth-grade students I'd known as friends and classmates over at Williams School had moved along with me to Port School. There was a protective shield covering me with the number of kids I perceived as being on my side. That was what I thought. That made me feel better, and with the urging of my mother that anything new takes time to get used to, I eventually became comfortable in my surroundings. The main reason for my having adjusted so well focused on my close friendship with Eddie Howard, the kid who'd gotten me into some trouble on the very first day of class. He was the joker of the class. He wasn't as bad as I first had pictured him to be. Yes, he was funny, and definitely funny-looking. But Eddie was easy to be with. Comforting was the perfect word. I always acted myself with him. The astonishing fact that Miss Potter allowed us to stay seated next to one another made us behave. We were extremely careful. We didn't want to be separated. Eddie only made faces or said nutty things when Miss Potter was out of the room, an intelligent move on his part.

Because of their insistence, my attention was drawn toward two girls in my class. "Ben, when you go from one school to another," my mother warned me the week before I began attending Port School, "there will be certain things and surprises that you'll be faced with. Please be aware of this and always be prepared, okay? They're sneaky in nature and will appear without you ever knowing it. You'll be in for a shock if you haven't put up any guards to protect yourself. You can't trust everyone." So I learned from meeting those girls.

Yvette and Alice were typical "Port girls." The people from this section of town differed from the East Danvers folks. Unlike the other sections of town, all the houses in the Port were clustered together, causing a lot of people to reside in a small area. If a neighbor had a cold, chances were the person next door practically heard the coughing and sneezing from his house. Given that proximity, "the wharf rats," as Port people were called from that working community, never were safe from anyone's knowing their personal business. Not to mention that many unsavory jokes often circulated around Danvers concerning the backwardness of the wharf rats. There were also many rumors. The Port people supposedly possessed a strong character, a certain togetherness that gave them a reputation of being livelier and spunkier. They without fail told you exactly what was on their minds. The place was bustling with factories, which meant it was a blue-collar haven. Creese and Cook, an enormous old building that housed hundreds of workers, anchored the main thoroughfare, Water Street, and was a sure sign that there were few softies. They were rough and ready people, the grapevine had it. And Port History presented the proud facts of those individuals who had overcome a poorer background to become professors, teachers, and successful businessmen. Their sports figures excelled on the fields and courts of Danvers. They were legendary. I remembered as an impressionable youngster attending a Twilight League game between Ferncroft and Port in the late 40s how fiercely contested it was. All the geographical areas of Danvers boasted of their stars and luminaries, but, indisputably, the Port light was always brighter.

Yvette and Alice sat beside each other at the back of Miss Potter's classroom. Yvette was a black-haired, dark-skinned girl who had a definite attitude, one that bowled a boy over if he weren't careful. She was cute in a cautionary way. I noticed her the first day of school. I was sure most boys noticed her. She looked like an Indian girl, one who was the daughter of Chief Red Foot in one of those cowboy movies I was so fond of. I knew that had I lived on that reservation I would've become very friendly with the chief. I was struck by the way Yvette kept looking at me with that smirk of hers. It annoyed me, but it soon became something I would've missed had she stopped doing it for very long. Fortunately for my sake she didn't stop.

Alice was the exact opposite of her flashy friend. Her skin was very fair and had such a delicate texture to it that she must've burned terribly in the summer. The sun would wreak havoc on her in no time. And her hair was a silky blonde with a certain glow to it. Add that to the fact that she had beautiful blue eyes and any boy who liked girls just a little couldn't help but stare at her. But the one thing about Alice that attracted me the most was her shyness. It wasn't false. She really had trouble even looking at boys. I knew she was struggling in that department. I had trouble picturing her as being Yvette's chum. One clearly overpowered the other. But for some reason unknown to me, Alice didn't appear bothered at all by her friend's cockiness. I didn't know why but I didn't think I was good enough for either girl.

The two of them together reminded me so much of the Archie Comic Books. Yvette was "Veronica" in the comic strip, while Alice represented the perfect part for "Betty." Both girls were pretty and were friends. They stepped right into the pages and played the characters to perfection. The way the cartoonist portrayed the pair probably differed considerably, however, from the real Yvette and Alice. In that fantasy world, Veronica was the one who was sought after by many interested boys. Betty, meanwhile, stayed in the background, preferring to play second fiddle to her more popular friend. Given this scenario, most readers believed Betty was getting the short end of the stick. But it wasn't necessarily so. Sometimes the seconds won out over the firsts. Veronica wasn't immune from being devastated by some boy who, by some quirk of fate, chose somebody else over her. Anything was possible. My grandfather had always told me that. But I never seemed to understand that theory. Just like Betty in her relationship with Veronica in the comics, Alice didn't necessarily feel inferior to Yvette. Alice's being quiet and reserved didn't mean she didn't go after what she wanted. On the contrary, she had her own methods of achieving her goals. All this valuable information about the two girls came from Eddie. He was a true busybody. He lived down the street from Alice, had for years, and his mother was close to Yvette's mother. They'd gone through school together.

CHAPTER FIFTEEN

It didn't take Eddie Howard long to let me in on the secrets of the Port; within a week or two of knowing him, I'd learned the ins and outs of his beloved neighborhood.

"Most of the people here work at Creese and Cook," he said in an animated tone as we were sitting at the counter of McFadden's for an ice cream after school hours. He added, "There are a lot of pretty girls—wait, you'll see. Yvette, Judy, Bonnie, Alice, and Laurie are all pretty. My mother always tells me not to take girls seriously. I don't, anyway, Ben, if you know what I mean. I'd rather just screw around in school and play games at home—and I love Sandy Beach in the summer. I'm there all the time. You like the beach, don't you?" Eddie kept busy on his chocolate ice cream cone and in the meantime had also bought a Butterfingers to go along with it. My mother usually blasted me if I ate so much before supper. Eddie suddenly nudged me and said in an excited voice, "Want to know a real secret, Ben? Listen to this. You've heard of Louie's, right? They have the best pizza in the world. Boy, wait until you taste it. Everyone from all around comes there on Friday and Saturday nights. It's unbelievable." I listened to my new friend, eager to find out what he was about to tell me. "The locals all love the thin pizza; it's so steamy hot and crusty. But listen. Most of the men who go there talk about sports and get smashed on beer. My father likes it there, too. He's always there after a hard week at Creese and Cook. He comes home real tired from work. He's sweaty and mean. Sometimes he doesn't even eat supper. Then off he goes to Louie's, leaving my mother, my sister Susan and me at the kitchen table." Eddie made a fist and pretended to throw a punch at me. "My mother gets so angry at Dad that I'm afraid to be around her. But listen to this. After a few hours, Mom has me go after my father to Louie's. Boy, what a thrill! I can hardly wait for her to ask me. 'Go get your father, Eddie,' she yells, 'and don't come home without him.' I rush out of the house and head down River Street and turn on Water Street. I can hardly wait, Ben. I feel as if I'm escaping into the night. It only takes me a couple minutes to reach Louie's." Eddie winked sarcastically. "When I reach Louie's, get this. I go in the back way, where all the men are sitting on the stools at the bar. I see my father but don't go to him right away. I'm a smart kid, you know. I'm not as stupid as I look." Eddie laughed out loud, almost choking in the bargain. "The men are swearing like mad, Ben, and they're talking about women, too. It makes me feel like a grown-up." Eddie finished his story by telling me that he finally managed successfully to get his father home safely.

Alice was coy in her dealings with boys. At first, before I knew her, I never realized how clever she really was. To almost all the students at Port School who were more than simply acquainted with her, compared to the obstreperous Yvette she was a sweet, mild-mannered girl who didn't dare step beyond the bounds of normal, acceptable behavior. I wasn't sure of anyone, anyway. Bampy and Mom had taught me not to assume anything. Given the motives and needs involved, some people went to extraordinary measures. So it was with the blonde, blue-eyed Alice. I soon discovered she used Lois as the necessary go-between to get her point across, to do her dirty work.

During one recess period, Lois approached me in the playground abutting the school. Did I know Alice had been absent a couple of days? I did, only because Yvette wasn't herself without her friend around. According to Lois, Alice was sick with a disease no one was able to pinpoint. The family doctor had been to her house and, after examining the young patient, was perplexed as to what was causing her to have such a high fever. Lois seemed upset as she related this tragic information to me. Maybe, she suggested, I should call Alice to find out how she was doing. It certainly wouldn't hurt; she'd be happy to hear from me.

Unknown to me at the time, I was the only student whom Lois had told this to. I was bothered by the news, by the impending catastrophe. I didn't know Alice but I knew of her. She sat in the back of the classroom. I was confused as to what to do. When I went home that afternoon, I asked my mother what I should do. Lois had given me Alice's telephone number on a tiny slip of paper. I thought everything was on the level. Girls at Williams School had never shown any interest in me. Even if they had, I never noticed it. Other than that blonde woman on the bus, when it came to girls, I didn't pay much attention. After all, I'd been mesmerized by a beautiful woman, not a girl. Playing ball and hanging around the neighborhood with Kenny had been my major concerns. And dice baseball. Only lover-boy Joey Buccella had any experience with girls. And he was out of commission, all the way in New Mexico. That evening, while alone with Mom, I told her the story, how Lois had informed me of Alice's illness.

"You've got to do the right thing, Ben," she advised me. "I brought you up to be kind and considerate to people. Call Alice immediately and see how she's doing, how she feels," my mother said. "It isn't wrong for you to do that. It's a good move on your part, Ben, okay? It may lift Alice's spirits. The poor girl maybe is very sick."

After supper that evening, I called Alice. I was jittery as the phone rang up the number. I agonized as it rang three times. Finally a soft-sounding female voice answered. "Hello," someone said. Momentarily I had a blank feeling.

"Is this Alice?" I asked, "the girl at Port School?"

"Yes, it is," she said. " Who is this, may I ask?"

My heart was beating like mad as I blurted out, "This is Ben. Ben Robblee. You know, the kid who sits up front beside Eddie Howard." Alice started to cough a little and murmured, "Oh, what a surprise. How nice. Yes, I know who you are, Ben. You're the boy with the real curly hair, aren't you? Yvette and I have talked about you. You're from East Danvers, right?" I didn't understand how she knew about me; I'd hardly said a word since going to Port School.

"I called you, Alice, because I heard from Lois that you're very sick. You don't mind, do you?"

Moments passed before she answered, "No, no, I'm very happy you called. You're the first one to call me. Wow, it's wonderful, Ben."

The conversation continued for a few minutes. Alice told me she was feeling better, and would I enjoy coming over to her house to see her in a few days or so, when she was completely well. She'd make me some of her special chocolate chip cookies and we'd listen to her forty-five-speed records. She wanted to show me how much she appreciated my concern over her health. Well, I was overcome with joy; never had I expected such an exciting thing to happen to me. I was so surprised by Alice's reaction to my phone call and to her invitation that I didn't speak for several seconds. It was a numb feeling that left me in a state of euphoria. No girl had ever talked to me like that before. Yes, I agreed to come over to see her whenever she wanted me to, and yes, I loved chocolate chip cookies more than anything. When I put the phone back down on the receiver, I sat there for several minutes so stunned that I didn't get right to sleep that night. When my mother finally heard me moving around in the hallway real late (it was almost midnight), she came downstairs and offered, "What are you doing, Ben? Look how late it is. Gracious, get to bed before your father hears us." I got a little scared and said, "Sure, Mom, I'm sorry," and went back to my room to try to get to sleep.

I never pictured myself as being "Archie" in the comic books. He was the main guy. Veronica and Betty were constantly pursuing him. It was an ideal situation. I didn't fit the part. In the first four grades I was, I suppose, reasonably popular with most of the kids at Williams School. But I certainly hadn't awakened yet when it came to girls. Of course, I was definitely stuck on Miss Kent. But that was the extent of any thinking I did concerning the opposite sex. I remembered, though, when I was four or five, I once picked up one of the magazines on the living-room table. I caught a glimpse of a picture of a woman wearing a bright-red bathing suit. The photo covered the whole page. The young model was sitting on the sand at a beach, which seemed silly to me at the time. Why did a magazine show a woman in a stupid bathing suit? During the few times I opened any magazines I only saw ads for such things as dress shirts or shoes or new cars. I never paid any attention to the particular names of the products. There always were copies of *Good Housekeeping* and *Redbook* around for us to look at because my mother subscribed to many magazines. Up to and including my years at Williams School, I didn't give much thought to girls.

CHAPTER SIXTEEN

Alice returned to school the following week. She looked great to me, as if she hadn't been sick at all. Her blonde hair glowed against the light and she looked happy to be back with her friends. Yvette made a big deal out of her return. She hugged Alice and giggled a lot. Other than that, everything was back to normal. Everything, that is, but my frame of mind. I was fidgety. I wanted to see Alice in private to speak to her. I never recalled feeling that way before. I was impatient and I trembled plus I kept turning around in class and looking toward the back of the room. She sat there, smiling at me. I wondered if something wonderful was happening between us. That idea made me tingle inside. Miss Potter could've been speaking in Italian and I wouldn't have noticed it. And Eddie just stared at me from his seat as if he were totally confused. I was sure he suspected something was up but he didn't know what. His confusion as to my sudden change in behavior grew as lunchtime neared. In spite of his staring at me, thus indirectly hinting for me to reveal some monumental secret to him, some new gossip, I didn't budge. I wasn't going to, either. I agonized over whether Alice was thinking about me as much as I was thinking about her. If she was, things were looking up. It reminded me of Joey Buccella. What would Joey have done if he'd been in my position?

As the bell rang, signaling the time for lunch, I turned around suddenly to see if Alice was still in her seat. She was. Good. I was breathless and found it difficult to wait any longer. I remembered precisely what Lois had instructed me to do that morning before school had begun. I'd met her outside of the room across the hall; she didn't have the same fifth-grade teacher as Alice and I did.

"At lunchtime, Ben, go outside your room after everyone has eaten, but don't let anyone see you. Pretend that you and Alice aren't going to meet, okay? Give Alice a minute to go outside for recess. She'll run to the far side of the building and stand in the corner where the front steps are and wait for you there. And Ben," Lois begged, further stressing a point. "Please don't tell anyone about this."

I had to get rid of Eddie, which was a major hurdle. He was bugging me to death, wanting to know what was what. Why was I behaving like this? It was one of the few times I went out of my way to be a stinker, but I had to protect myself. I made it clear to my friend that nothing was going on, that I wasn't going to spend the recess period with him. I disappeared quickly down the stairs to the first floor and found my way around the building to Alice. She was standing exactly where Lois said she'd be.

I didn't know what to say. I kept looking at her as if I couldn't believe that it was a girl who was facing me.

She seemed a little nervous; sometimes she'd gaze toward the street. I was unable to comprehend what had suddenly come over me. All I understood for certain was that I was flustered to be standing next to her. Sometimes words only complicated things. However, I realized that I had to speak soon since only fifteen minutes remained before the bell rang, ordering us back into the building for class. I kept imagining that Eddie, in his own sneaky way, might be looking for me.

"How are you feeling?" I finally asked, struggling a bit. "Why did you want to see me, Alice?" I wanted desperately to find out why she'd wanted me to call her.

The poor girl seemed on the verge of tears and for a moment looked down at the ground. Then, looking up, she lamented, "I'm feeling much better, thank you. I want you to know something. Please try to understand, Ben. This is going to be very difficult for me to explain and it might make you hate me. Please don't."

Alice, hesitating, revealed something shocking. All her emotions came spilling out in one big dose. "I want to sincerely apologize to you. Lois and I invented the whole story up to get your attention, Ben. Silly, huh? I had a bad cold but I wasn't really as sick as Lois said. It was nothing serious—no, it was all made up. That's it. I'm so sorry," she said, as tears appeared. "I just wanted to see you. I liked you from the first day of school. I know it sounds crazy but I like your curly hair and your eyes." She grinned, causing her to hiccup along with her crying. "Please don't be angry with me."

It wasn't in my nature to get angry with anyone, especially a girl. At that instant I felt very special. Someone had gone through all that for me? No girl had ever been even slightly forward with me. In fact, that was the first time I'd been interested in a girl at all. Since I was only in the fifth grade, it frightened me a little. I stood there, determined to be understanding and patient with Alice. Mom and Bampy had instilled those qualities in me. I didn't want to hurt her feelings; nonetheless, I was puzzled.

Alice and Lois certainly had succeeded in their plan. The next morning outside the schoolyard Alice tapped me on the shoulder and quietly said, "I hope we're friends, Ben. You're not mad at me, are you?"

I shook my head no.

"Good," she beamed. "It would bother me if you were. I'm so glad you're here at Port School. Before long maybe you'll be a real Port person," she asserted, putting her hands to her mouth to hold back her giggling. "And don't worry about Lois, she's a close buddy of mine. You can trust her not to spill the beans, okay? I never would've gone through our plan without her. She's a genius, you know. My other friend, Yvette, is a lot different. That's why I didn't ask her for help. She knows nothing about it, so please keep still." Again Alice put her hands to her mouth. "I'm sorry it happened, Ben, but it's over now. The whole thing was ridiculous, I know. Are you my friend? If so, why don't you come over to my house some afternoon and we can have some fun. My mother said it's okay."

I was even more surprised when she told me that Lois was Elaine Warner's friend. Elaine, whom I didn't see as much because she was going to a nearby private school, had spoken highly of me. "Ben's a great kid," Elaine had confirmed to Lois while the two girls were attending dance class. They were close pals. "Tell your friend Alice that he was a good friend of mine at Williams School. She can't go wrong with him." I stood there, nonplused.

It was time for the bell to ring. I looked at Alice admiringly and said, "Of course I'll be your friend, starting right this second. Yes, I'd like very much to visit you whenever you say it's okay. And don't forget, Alice, about the chocolate chip cookies." I gave her a little wink and was overjoyed at what was happening to me. I wasn't the type of kid who spoke out of line. Perhaps I was too polite. I never gave an opinion about anything or anybody if it entailed hurting anyone's feelings. Even if I strongly disagreed with somebody over something we were discussing, I allowed that person to get it out of his system unhampered.

There was nothing to forgive Alice for. The way I saw it, any girl who had thought up such a plan as she and Lois had, deserved much credit. It amounted to what the older kids in junior high and high school referred to as "a crush." Boy, I had it worse than Alice did.

I was so thrilled over the prospect of seeing Alice outside of school that I became impatient. I thought, what if we decided to walk to McFadden's Variety and Luncheon at the corner of Water Street and River Street to get something to eat? She lived right down River Street, heading toward Sandy Beach. But Eddie lived right down the street from her.

"I have to tell my friend Eddie about us, Alice. Sooner or later he'll find out anyway. He's a real snoop, you know. It's silly to keep it a secret. And, anyway, sometime we can go and visit him too, if it's all right with you." I figured it was possible to accomplish two things at once if I visited Eddie after seeing Alice.

"That sounds great," Alice agreed. "Why not tell Eddie, why not tell the whole world! We aren't doing anything wrong."

The bell rang for us to return to class; everything had gone perfectly between us. We'd gotten along extremely well without a hitch. Nothing had blown up in my face. Seldom did things go that smoothly for me. For the next couple of hours Eddie didn't leave me alone. Since we were sitting side-by-side, there was nothing I could do to prevent him from bothering me. Eddie was going to be Eddie. I simply smiled and pointed to Miss Potter. That was a warning to keep still. "Shut up," I whispered. "Wait until the end of class." That was enough for him to get the message. I did, however, keep turning around to look at Alice. I definitely didn't accomplish much that whole afternoon; I was having difficulty concentrating.

"Hey, Eddie," I called out loud after school had let out. He was walking about ten yards in front of me. Outside, I confessed to him. "Yes, Alice and I are friends now. Don't make a production out of it, Eddie. I'll be going to her house once in a while, if it's okay with you, your Highness." Eddie began to roar, a hideous sound that reverberated throughout the Port. "Sure, it sounds great, Ben. I'm glad you told me, since I know everything," he bragged. "I'm the big cheese of the Port."

I went home that afternoon feeling content about my life.

My contentment was short-lived, however. Just when I was on a high, something sprang up to balance it off. Reality set in. My concern was my parents. What was I going to tell them about my friendship with Alice? Her parents had approved of the idea. Her mother had been the one who'd suggested that Alice invite me to their house sometime. I was troubled by the very thought of spilling it all out to my mother. As for my father, I wasn't sure.

Telling my mother anything about Alice and me was a big problem. I was going to play it safe. I decided to tell her that I had several friends from Port School. That covered everything and it wasn't a lie plus it added some drama to the whole arrangement. What about my father? Was I getting away with something untoward? The most important thing, however, was the feeling that I was doing something totally on my own. That I possessed such courage surprised me.

I always seemed to get wound up tight whenever something good was happening to me. I thought it would never last. It was a recurring fear of mine. Maybe I didn't believe that I deserved to be happy. Maybe I had an aversion to anything positive in my life. So it was with the blonde-haired, blue-eyed Alice. Being her friend was an excellent chance for me to start being my own kid. I dwelled on the thought that some boy would become jealous of what I had and try to take it away from me. Why didn't I enjoy the wonderful times when they were handed to me? I wanted the whole world to know that Alice was my friend. Conversely, I didn't want a soul to know about it. I was afraid my bubble would burst.

CHAPTER SEVENTEEN

The following days were conflicting ones for me. I was seeing Alice in school as much as possible and still having lots of fun with Eddie. Everything as far as school was concerned was going well. But at home it was entirely different. I was unsettled. My mother always had a knack of sniffing something out that was happening in my life. She didn't say much to me. But she noticed how quiet I'd become. I tried to act as if everything were normal. Even though that was difficult, I was succeeding to some extent. It didn't make any difference how I behaved in front of my two brothers and my father. They were too disinterested in me to notice anything.

"Are you feeling all right, Ben?" my mother inquired late one afternoon. "You seem upset over something. You've been very quiet lately." She came over to me and touched my forehead. "No, you don't have a temperature. What's going on with you? Do you want to tell me something about school?"

"No, Mom, nothing's wrong. Really, believe me. Everything at school is good. I don't know what to say. Please don't worry about me—I'm not a baby."

"I know that—I'm just concerned, that's all."

Suddenly something hit me like a block of bricks against the middle of my skull. How was I going to get to Alice's house or to Eddie's? I didn't have the means of going that far; it was a considerable distance, about two miles, from East Danvers to the Port. My father wasn't always available, not to mention the fact that I didn't want him to know about anything. At first I became panicky. After all, I wasn't a long-distance runner. I had to go down Cardinal Road, which was a hill, then all the way along Elliott Street and Williams School. Finally, a left on Liberty Street and another quarter mile and finally to McFadden's on River Street where Alice and Eddie lived and the trip was completed. If I walked it, I would have to take along a backpack with a couple sandwiches to avoid starving to death.

I sat alone in my room listening to the radio. I tried to figure out how to solve my dilemma; I was depressed. There had to be somebody who was able to suggest a brainstorm. It struck me as odd that I hadn't thought about the distance factor when I'd first met Alice that day after lunch. I'd been in dreamland, too excited over our conversation. Never had it dawned on me that she practically lived in another country. Maybe I could sprout wings and fly over Williams School and the Danvers River in order to reach her house. Sitting there on my bed, I started to feel sorry for myself.

The first thing I did was to phone my grandfather. Since he couldn't hear well, my grandmother, as always, answered the call. I immediately asked for her permission to come over that Saturday to be with them. It was urgent but I didn't tell her that. She said yes. They were always glad to see me. She enjoyed cooking for anyone who came to her house. I looked forward to those vanilla cupcakes covered with fresh chocolate frosting.

On that Saturday, Nanny greeted me at the front door. She was curious as to why I'd called her. "My sweet Ben, when you called I noticed that you sounded nervous. Why did you call? Is anything wrong, dear? Please tell your grandma." She was wearing an old housedress that reached all the way down to her laced black shoes and her hands had some flour splattered on them. During the many years I spent at my grandparents' place I noticed that they were the two most covered-up people I ever knew. Seldom did I see their arms or their legs. And Grandma Foster didn't appear tired from all that housework. Perhaps that was what kept her going. If she had plunged herself into a soft chair, she probably would've fallen asleep for days, or never awakened.

The amazing thing was I hadn't said one thing to her about what was on my mind. Just like her daughter often did, my grandmother guessed something was bothering her grandson.

"There is something sort of serious bothering me,

Nanny," I admitted, "but I want to tell Bampy first. We're close buddies and he'll understand."

She peered at me as if she were wondering why she couldn't help me. She seemed a bit upset over what I'd said. I knew that I shouldn't have said anything, but unfortunately I had. Usually I was too deliberate in my conversations with people but that time I wasn't.

Nanny, looking cross, approached the kitchen chair on which I was sitting. Her face had reddened and had an unaccustomed, mean look to it. She started to grind her teeth, displaying her taut cheek muscles.

"What do you mean, Ben, by insinuating that I can't help you with your problems?" She was ticked off; her arms were flaring about as she paced around the kitchen floor. "If you think for one minute, boy, that Pa can help you more than I can, you're sadly mistaken. What are you, in never-never land? What does your grandpa know about solving anything, huh? Absolutely nothing." I thought Nanny was going to explode at any second. It was the most put out I'd ever seen her. She had stopped everything to let me have it right between the eyes. All I dared to do was absolutely nothing. I just sat there looking helpless. "Pa's every need in life has been prepared and supplied by me, boy. He's never wanted for anything." Not even the sun shining in through the kitchen window was an antidote to the dark mood being caused by Nanny's loud voice. She didn't stop her tirade, on and on it went. "Why, I've been a wife, a maid, a housekeeper, a nurse—everything to him over the years.

He's been living in total comfort." She began to laugh sarcastically, as if she were the only one in the room.

I sat there, stunned over what had suddenly happened. I didn't know what to make of it. She had let out all her feelings in one big swoop. Bette Davis possessed no acting talent compared to her. Fifty-two years of an up-and-down marriage had been released in five minutes.

It took her an hour to get over it and then, to my surprise, she caressed and kissed me several times on the forehead as if nothing had happened at all. I never forgot that incident.

It was much later, after many years and several discussions with Aunt Helen, that I was informed of the full ramifications of what had transpired way back on that day in the kitchen with my grandmother. Nanny had lived a very difficult life, indeed; at times it'd been downright miserable for her.

My grandfather, "good old Percy," had a great deal of faith in my father. So to skirt around any issue that involved Dad was futile. The main thing here was that I had to respect and understand Bampy's feelings toward Dad. I didn't understand all the inner workings of what this was all about, but I had a pretty good idea. I'd seen the two of them together many times and learned a few things. I didn't presume, because I was so close to the old guy, he'd side with me automatically over my father. My grandfather was loyal toward both of us. Nonetheless I didn't dare to take a chance that he was more loyal toward me. Bampy was an old man who'd lived through several generations, had experienced and seen more of life than I ever could imagine. My approach, since my aim was to get something of value out of our meeting, had to be delicate yet target in on what I really wanted. I wanted to be able to see Alice and Eddie. I didn't want my grandfather to know too much about the situation. Alice was constantly on my mind. Being able to get to the Port was my great concern. To accomplish that end I needed the means to get back and forth to see my friends. I wasn't asking for the world here. I did see them plenty of times during school. The bus leaving the Port Corner by the Baptist church on High Street came from Danvers Square at three-fifteen every day. Since I got out of school at two-thirty I only had forty-five minutes to be with Alice or Eddie.

I'd informed Alice of my meeting with my grandfather on Friday, the day before the actual event. "I don't see how I can come to your house if I don't have a ride," I moaned. We were walking toward McFadden's right after school. Alice was humming a tune, the name of which I didn't know.

"What do you mean, Ben? That's no problem. I told you my mother is available sometimes to give you a ride home if you don't have one. It isn't a biggie. She's heard a lot of good things about your family and is glad I have a new friend, especially because it's you. I understand you're worried about it, but don't be."

"But I am worried. I want to do things for myself. I hate depending on my parents or any adults for anything."

"I'm happy to see you whenever I can, Ben, even if it's

only once a week. Everything will work out, okay?"

I felt relieved as we entered McFadden's and I tried to shake off my concern over the matter. Things always lingered with me, wouldn't let go.

My grandfather walked slowly into the kitchen where I was sitting. I'd been waiting impatiently for him. Nanny was busy in the pantry fixing something to eat. I got up quickly from the chair and gave him a big hug.

"Bampy," I said, "I'd like to talk to you."

"Sure," he said.

I gestured toward the living room—hinting that I wanted to converse with him alone. He nodded and I followed him through the dining room into the living room. All the furniture was simple: a huge brown corduroy divan, a large walnut desk and straight chair, another chair that rocked and had a smooth mahogany finish to it, and an enormous easy chair dominating the far corner of the room near the front window. There was nothing fancy about the place; it felt as if its occupants had lived there forever.

Bampy sat down in the easy chair in the corner. Everything he did, it seemed, took forever. I knew that our conversation wouldn't take place until he was finished doing what he had to do, until he was good and ready for me. He settled himself into the chair and stared momentarily outside the window into the street. The brightness confronted him, was a shock to his system, making him use his hands as a visor to protect his eyes. After a few moments, after he'd regained his visual composure, he reached for one of the many pipes resting on a circular stand beside the chair. He was painfully meticulous as not to disrupt any of the other pipes. After a process of scraping clean the black pipe he'd chosen, he filled it with fresh aromatic tobacco from a pouch that was resting nearby. After all this, he lit the pipe with a match and started to puff away. What a scene it was!

Within the space of two or three minutes, a thick film of smoke virtually enveloped his head. Gray clouds spread around the chair. A pleasant, hypnotic odor spread throughout the whole room. It appeared as if Bampy were a fire chief in the midst of a major conflagration; it made me feel closer to him. I didn't know how the old man was able to breathe. But the fog-like effect caused by the incinerated tobacco in the pipe seemed to enable him to be even more contented than if he'd been there surrounded by clear, clean air. The smoke seemed to act like oxygen. His eyes were flickering, as if he were in deep thought over something in his past. Perhaps he was back living in his thirties when he was manager of Swift's, a prominent meat business that had been in operation for years on the North Shore and beyond. Maybe he was dreaming about the difficult time he'd once related to me, when he first came to Salem by himself and had struggled to make a living. Or possibly he was thinking of his days in Wolfeboro, New Hampshire, sitting beside his sweetheart (soon to be his wife) in the horse-drawn carriage about to take them on a romantic evening ride. I'd seen a picture in my grandparents' attic of Nanny as a young woman: wearing one of those old dresses with frills on the sleeves and a white scarf encircling her neck, and with long hair flowing neatly about the sides of her face, she looked stunning.

My grandfather finished smoking his pipe. The living room smelled of sweet tobacco. In order to face him as we talked I went over and sat on the stool that matched his easy chair. It wasn't that Bampy was rude or anything, but he was so preoccupied with himself that it was necessary for me to enter his world if I wanted to talk to him. Once I got his attention everything seemed to fall into place. He was probably like this because of his hearing impairment. At least that's what my grandmother told me. Sometimes, she said, she failed to get his attention and she'd been married to him forever. Perhaps it was just as well. They were so familiar with one another that anything that they had to say to each other had already been gone over a thousand times.

"So, how's everything with you, Ben?" Bampy put forth. "Your grandmother told me you called."

"Yes, I did. Did she say anything else?"

"No, was she supposed to?" he asked.

"I was in a hurry to see you, Bampy. I think Nanny thinks I'm all nerved up over something."

He studied me and added, "Oh, is there anything upsetting you?"

"Yes, in a way there is."

Grandpa Foster sat back in his chair and placed his

hands behind his head. When he did that, I interpreted that particular move as his way of telling me that he was going to pay strict attention.

"You see, I've got new friends at Port School. At first I had some trouble there but now everything has cleared up. It's a lot different than Williams School, a lot harder. It's bigger and I don't know most of the kids. Mom told me to be patient."

"It sounds pretty typical to me, Ben. Anything new takes time to get used to."

"Yes, I guess you're right, but it's not really that. You see, Port School is a long way from our house and I want to see my friends more. I usually take a bus to and from school or Dad drives me in the morning if he has time. I like the bus much better."

"Then what's the problem?"

"I don't want to depend all the time on him—or anyone. I want to come and go as I please," I stressed, raising my voice a bit.

"Is there a young girl you like, Ben?"

I looked down, felt embarrassed by his question. "Well, in a way, yes, but I also have a close friend named Eddie. I've known him a lot longer than the girl."

Bampy chuckled before speaking. "I understand. I'm getting by all this chatter between us that you wish to see that girl and what's his name, oh yes, Eddie, on the weekends. Am I right?"

"How'd you know that, Bampy?"

"I think I've lived a little longer than you, Ben."

"Then what do you think I should do, huh?" I pulled the footstool closer to him.

"Let's see, my boy," he pondered, rubbing his chin. He was the cleanest-shaved man I'd ever seen. His face was as smooth as mine.

"How are you and your father getting along lately?"

"What do you mean? I suppose about the same. You must know, don't you?"

"I suppose I do, Ben, but I think you're not even trying to make things better between the two of you. Are you?"

"Sometimes I don't think he likes me at all. He's always—you know."

"I'm not sure I do know, but I think I get the drift of what you're saying, my boy."

"Then what can I do? I need a way of getting back and forth to the Port. What's that got to do with my father?"

"Ben, for goodness sake. You're not stupid. It's got everything in the world to do with him. He's the one who can solve your problem and you can't even see it."

"He can? How? What can Dad do that'll help me?"

"Think, my boy. Think. If you ask him, maybe he'll buy you a new bike. But remember, you don't get something for nothing, you know."

"What do you mean?"

"I mean you must tell him in exchange for the bike you'll do chores around the house for him and your mother. You get it?"

"Wow, I never thought about that. How come?"

"Because you were too worried about your problem, that's why. What do you think about my suggestion?"

"It's unbelievable, Bampy. I hope Dad goes along with your idea."

"He will, believe me. He's not the monster you think he is. Believe it or not, my boy, he's a decent man. He loves you as much as he loves Scott and Andy."

"I don't know about that," I said.

"He does. By the way, you must take special care of the bike. And another thing is important, my boy. Don't tell him why you want the bike. Remember, he doesn't have to know the reason. Just tell him it's for getting around, for making things easier for you. He won't have to cart you all over Danvers, anymore."

I felt so relieved I almost cried. "Wow, thanks, Bampy!"

He gave me a big hug and offered one last bit of advice. "You don't have to tell anyone your personal business, remember that. The less you open that trap of yours the better. You get it? And everything in your life isn't a do-or-die situation. Take it easy, for goodness sake, okay? Your father isn't against you. He's your friend. Always remember that, too."

Bampy slapped me on the back, then we returned to the kitchen. One thing was for sure: I had a lot on my mind after our conversation.

CHAPTER EIGHTEEN

When I left my grandparents' house in North Salem that evening, I certainly was upbeat. Yet, on the ride home with my father, I suddenly became quiet. I didn't say a word. After all, Bampy and I had just talked about him at length. Somehow, I didn't know why, but a huge feeling of guilt took control of me, as if I'd been a traitor to my own Dad. There he was, picking me up and driving me home, something he'd been doing for a long time. I kept thinking about what my grandfather had said.

I waited until the next day, a Sunday, to ask Dad about the bicycle. It was strange, but as much as I wanted it, my mind wasn't as set on having it as it'd been before that visit with Bampy. I was consumed with what the old man had said about my father. That he was "a good man" seemed to stick to me like Elmer's Glue. In retrospect, I was stubborn and proud. My minister at church, Dr. Samuel Petersen, had once preached in one of his sermons, "To do unto others as you would have them do unto you." Why didn't my father adhere to that policy? Or was it I who didn't adhere to it? That was something for me to think about.

The next afternoon I went to my father and asked him

outright. I was very jittery.

"Dad, I want to talk to you about something real important," I began, "I've been thinking about it for a couple weeks now." I was afraid to look at him.

My father put down a sports magazine he was reading and looked at me. He was sitting in the big yellow easy chair that was perpetually reserved for him. None of us ever dared get near that chair when Dad was around. If by chance he caught one of his three sons ensconced in it, he stared him down and waved his right arm. The message was clear: get out of that chair, pronto.

"Yes, Ben, what has been on that busy mind of yours?"

"Well, Dad, I want to ask you for a real big favor. I hope you don't get mad at me. It's something I'd like you to get me," I said, forcing myself to look directly at him.

"What is it, Ben? If I can help, I'm willing to listen."

"I need something real bad. It means a lot to me. I'll take good care of it and I'll even do anything around the house you and Mom want me to."

He took an El Producto cigar out of a box nearby, quickly lit it with a match, and puffed ceremoniously on it a couple of times. A strong aroma immediately filled the area, causing me to cough. "I can't help you if I don't know what you're talking about, can I?"

"No, I suppose not, Dad. I need a bike real bad."

"Mm, a bike." A slight smile appeared on his face, giving me some hope.

"Yes, a bike. You see it'll help me get around easier and

you won't have to drive me everywhere."

"I see, Ben. Yes, I don't think that'll be a problem. Sure, I'll buy you a bike, but that means you'll always have to use care when riding it. Always play it safe, Ben. Is that clear?" My father's smile became broader; frankly, I didn't believe what I'd just heard. "Actually I once had a bike, too, Ben, so I know what it means to be a boy who wants something as if his life depended on it. My father got me a used bike when I was about your age, but it wasn't bad. A bike is a bike."

Later that evening I sat on my bed, thinking. In a way, I felt like a heel. It was as if I were one of the East Danvers Red Sox in dire need of a uniform or a pair of sneakers and my father had come through for me. He was again extending help to someone and it happened to be me. The one thing that made me the happiest that afternoon was when I hugged him for what he'd done for me. Very seldom did that occur.

On Monday, at recess, I related the good news to Alice. I'd told Eddie about it before school had begun. Both of them were happy to hear my father was going to get me a bike. Alice was happier for me than she was for herself. I noticed she'd become friendly with Eddie because she realized he was my buddy. Everything was coming together. I explained I'd done exactly what my grandfather had advised me to do. Alice agreed with me that I should listen to him all the time. She said that everyone should have someone to run to in an emergency. She also reminded me that she'd tried to instill within me a feeling of calm over the whole situation. She was always telling me to take it easy. Everything eventually worked out. Her statement was so coincidental in that my grandmother's favorite motto was "patience is a virtue." After all, she was married to Bampy. I easily understood how she'd come up with that saying. It was odd, but when I was a kid, I didn't think older people knew anything. The opposite was true. I believed the world revolved around me; there was nothing I didn't know.

Alice was quite mature for her age. She didn't act like a fifth-grader. I swore she was almost as smart as my mother was. She had an answer for most questions. She seemed capable of reading my mind. And on top of that, she was pretty. Alice had been brought up in an intelligent family, one that savored the ideal of scholarship. Her father was an engineer at a big company and her mother was a psychologist of some kind. A few kids sometimes joked with her over the fact that she lived in the Port. How had she ended up there? Why didn't she live in Wenham or Manchester, communities that were more upscale? She only laughed it off. She retorted that there were plenty of nice people in the Port, too. They all weren't rough-and-ready folks. Besides, her parents wanted her to grow up in a more down-to-earth environment. However, how was it that she didn't get swallowed up in all that coarseness? I was sure there was a genius or two living in the Port, even though it was the poorest section of town.

The new bicycle turned out to be a bright red 1948

Road Master Luxury Liner, a real beauty. Upon my first seeing it, I was so excited that it was difficult for me not to break out crying. I was tense as I mounted it for the first time in front of my father. I didn't believe the bike belonged to me. The most dominant thought I was burdened with was the overwhelming contrition I felt concerning Dad. As I took my bicycle out for its first spin up and down Hillcrest Road I wondered, how did a kid even begin to deal with the negative feelings he had for someone, especially his father, when the person he resented had done something so powerfully positive for him? Everything for me seemed to be split unfairly into two broken pieces. There was one good piece and one bad piece. They never came together to form a whole piece. I was always struggling with this problem. Alice had the right idea. She maintained that I should relax and not get nervous over things. Everything would be fine in the end. But it wasn't that easy for me to do. Nothing ever was.

The first time I rode my bike to the Port to visit Alice was an invigorating experience. I felt independent as I went by Williams School on Elliott Street and then finished the route on Liberty Street. I wasn't dependent anymore, for the most part, on my father for transportation. And even though it was difficult for me to rid myself of all negative thoughts, I was determined to do so.

CHAPTER NINETEEN

My fifth-grade year went as well as expected. There were a few hair-raising incidents that flared up that threw me for a loop. Alice and I became closer friends and I still hung around with Eddie. He had replaced Kenny as my closest buddy. Eventually my parents found out about my seeing both Alice and Eddie at their respective houses. Neither one was particularly concerned over my having friends, as long as they were good kids. I was somewhat surprised my father never voiced any criticism whatsoever over my being friendly with a girl. If my mother objected, I never knew about it.

On the way home from those visits I left just before it started to get too dark. I was very careful while riding my bike down the length of Liberty Street. I envisioned some creepy figure darting out of nowhere and beating me half to death. So it took considerable courage to pass through that area. After I took a right to go down Elliott Street, the main street, I had to be cautious not to get clipped by some crazy driver.

There were two characters, Buster Kemper and Bruce Hatfield, during my fifth-grade year in Miss Potter's class that surfaced and became my foes, students who were placed there, or so I believed, for the sole purpose of disrupting my life at Port School. Buster, whose bark was far greater than his bite, as it later turned out, wasn't as harmful to me as Bruce was. The Kemper kid actually ended up being helpful to my cause in dealing with the treacherous Hatfield. It was strange the way things unwound. I wasn't ready to confront these guys. Outside of that initial confrontation with the blond kid, Charlie, way back on the first day of school in September, I'd been fortunate in having avoided any further scrapes. I was proud of that—so far, so good. But, compared to that first minor event, which was kindergarten stuff, what was about to unfold was far worse. It was something that had far-reaching consequences in school and, possibly, at home.

Those two boys were bullies. There was a time in most boys' lives when they faced a situation that contained possible physical harm, at least with a few of the idiotic guys in the school. Fistfights outside on the grounds of Port School were common. The fights invariably involved a nice kid bent on doing well in school against a tough kid who was an unhappy thug. Mom explained to me that it wasn't always the miserable kid's fault for being that way, but other times it was because he was simply an awful person, a jerk.

The boys from Port School definitely didn't like the boys from East Danvers. That was a given. At least that was the case in the beginning. We were the spoiled brats who had more money and more things. However, there was one factor the Port kids failed miserably in understanding. They were part of a much more cohesive community where there existed more loyalty among the citizens. The Port was a more open society where the locals were familiar with one another; East Danvers was more private. The Port possessed more get-up-and-go, an aura about it. In a way, I wished I'd been brought up there. As silly as it sounded, I believed if I had, I would've been more able to cope with my problems.

Buster Kemper was a tough-looking kid who lived on the other end of the same street as Eddie. Even though some boys feared him, he was very quiet. In the classroom he was considered a "slow student." He lived near McFadden's on the side of the street where a dozen or so houses were cramped together leading up to Sandy Beach. If you were looking for privacy, that wasn't the place to be. Buster lived in a large two-family dwelling that was owned by his parents. To look at him few had the insight to figure out that he came from a family that was fairly well off. Buster's actions belied his standing in the community. His older brother Skip was a member of the high school football team. Buster resembled his older sibling in that he was a muscular guy who seemed to be much bigger than the other boys. But that wasn't really true. Actually he had a swagger about him that made him appear bigger. He was sort of creepy-looking. And he wasn't the cleanest looking kid on the block, either. There was no mistake as to what his image was. He had an expression on his face that broadcast the message of "who is my next victim going to be." He ran around the schoolyard before the start of school or at recess chasing the most helpless looking slob he could catch. The most ironic twist to this outlandish behavior was that he was really a harmless kid. Buster never hurt anyone. That's what Eddie told me over and over. "Please believe me, Ben, the guy's okay. I know—I grew up with him. His parents are great." But that was difficult to believe. It was as if he didn't belong at Port School. Where he did belong I wasn't sure.

My first encounter with Buster happened during a recess period in November. It was getting much colder outside. Eddie and I were standing in the schoolyard. I was usually with Eddie whenever Alice and I weren't kidding around.

Buster barreled out of nowhere and hoisted me up in his arms in a bear hug. It happened so fast that I wasn't sure what had transpired. Wham, to the ground I went! I was so shocked by the impact that it took the breath out of me. Eddie just stood there laughing like a madman. Buster didn't say one stinking word. He simply wrapped his arms around me and grunted. That insanity concluded by Buster's rushing away almost as quickly as he'd come into contact with me. It probably took all of two minutes. Meanwhile Eddie couldn't maintain his composure. He kept laughing. He was my friend?

The Buster problem was an ongoing thing. Eddie once again was a big help by convincing me that Buster wasn't a direct threat to me. He'd known him for years and he didn't mean to cause physical harm to anyone. So, armed with that reassurance, I accepted Eddie's word and decided the best course of action at the time was to tolerate it. If Buster got out of hand then I'd be forced to do something about it. But what that was I didn't know.

After several days of Buster's chasing me all over the yard, it got to the point where I was actually beginning to get a momentary thrill out of that silly game. I was becoming addicted to Buster's antics. If, for some reason, he hadn't come around to bother me, then I became the instigator and egged him on until he acted.

Bruce Hatfield was the kind of kid who was devastating to come up against. He was extremely handsome and, like Joey Buccella of East Danvers fame, many girls were attracted to him. His thick brown hair, slicked back with hair tonic, and fine, angular features, along with his flair for dressing in expensive clothes, made him stand out among the students. But, unlike Joey, he acted as if he were superior—and most kids thought he was. He wasn't nice like Joey was. Underneath his unquestionable popularity there was a vindictive streak. Upon my first getting to know Eddie, he'd warned me about Bruce. He came from one of the most prominent families in the Port. Mr. Hatfield was a big deal, an executive at Creese and Cook who enjoyed throwing his weight around. Even though he was respected in some circles, he was feared even more in others. Bruce always had his father to back him up whenever he got into trouble, or so I heard. The combination of father and son seemed too formidable a duo for most to confront.

The problem was that Bruce seemed jealous of me.

There was no sensible reason whatsoever that he should've felt threatened by me. He was much better-looking and very self-assured. But there was one girl, Alice, whom I was friendly with—and he wasn't!

On the opposite side, there were many girls who had a crush on Bruce. Even though he was famous, or infamous, I didn't understand for the life of me why any girl would enjoy being around him. He was a certified threat. Of course, back when we were kids, both girls and boys only cared about looks. I often heard comments like, "Oh, don't you think he's cute," or, "Wow, what a doll she is."

Bruce had heard Alice and I were friends. He also knew that Yvette and Alice hung around together. That was where Eddie came in; he was aware of everything that was going on. He told me Bruce liked Alice and was furious that she and I were friends. Alice never would've had anything to do with kids like Bruce; she'd see through guys like him in a second.

One morning before school had begun, one of Bruce's friends told Eddie that Bruce wanted to fight me outside in the schoolyard. I was allowed to pick the time and day and he'd agree to it. I started to panic; I wanted the gossipy Eddie to look further into the matter. It wouldn't take my friend very long to know what was what.

I was correct. The next day Eddie said, "Bruce doesn't like the kids you hang around, Ben, especially the ones from East Danvers. The fool's spreading the word all around school that you're afraid of him and don't dare to face him in a fight."

After being notified of this, I didn't know what to think or do—but I felt as if I were backed up against the wall.

Alice and I were stunned, unable to think clearly. She was in tears over it. She said, sobbing, "I'm lost over this, Ben. I don't know what to do or where to turn. I've never felt like this before, ever."

Where could we go for advice?

After school the following day I suggested something to Alice while we were sitting in McFadden's. "I think we should include Eddie in on what we're going to do," I suggested. "This is a weird problem, Alice. It has to be clobbered head on, don't you think? We're dealing with a real rat here. Bruce is a dangerous guy! A lot of kids know about him and are scared to death of him."

"The funny thing is, Ben, we haven't done anything wrong at all. This all began out of nowhere. I don't get it—it isn't fair. I don't even know Bruce, but my mother, I think, must've heard of his parents." Alice was sipping a vanilla ice cream soda.

There were only two people, maybe three, who were able to give us good advice. The first individual we obviously thought of was Alice's mother. She was a psychologist and extremely smart. She certainly knew something about kids like Bruce.

In a situation like that it didn't make any sense for me to run to my father. Indeed, he had a tendency to go berserk over such matters. He'd probably run straight to Mr. Hatfield and give him the business, smack him right in the mouth. There was no way that Dad would've cared who Bruce's father was or how much clout he had in Danvers. In this regard I held my father in high esteem. He'd come forward to help Alice and me in the fix we were in. His family always came first; even Bampy said that. My father always came to his kids' rescue no matter what it did to his own reputation.

After mulling it over Alice and I decided the only person able to solve my problem was my grandfather. Bampy was methodical and his knowledge of how to treat people in both good and bad situations was unquestionable. He possessed the shrewdness to suggest tactics that were unorthodox and workable. The most important factor in our decision was that my grandfather wasn't directly involved in the matter. Alice and I were confident that things were looking up.

"I feel better about this," Alice assured me before heading home that afternoon.

"Me, too," I said.

CHAPTER TWENTY

The plan Bampy devised was simple and direct. I was to instruct Eddie to go to Buster's house and, in his own inimitable style, convince him to approach Bruce in the only way he knew how to approach anyone, using fear. Eddie had to explain to Buster the reason for his doing this. It was to be made clear to Buster that Bruce was a big nuisance who was causing a lot of problems with some of the kids. This had to be done as plainly as possible. Buster wasn't that intelligent, which further complicated my friend's go-between job. Eddie had to further elaborate that he and I considered Buster a good friend. Finally, it behooved Eddie to impress upon Buster that I was being hurt by what Bruce was saying about me in school.

The best time for Buster to get to Bruce, Bampy figured, was right after school when the two of them would be out in the open and alone. Bruce never would be expecting anything to happen. Buster was to follow his prey and when the troublemaker was the most vulnerable, when no one was near them, he was to pounce on him and let him have it. A few quick smashes to the body and face would suffice. But Buster shouldn't overdo it. Eddie had to instruct him to order Bruce to leave me alone and to stop talking about me. He had to put a real scare into Bruce. It had to stop immediately. If Buster didn't agree to that plan, then all bets were off and I had to come up with another scheme all over again. As a reward to Buster there was a week's supply of candy bars at McFadden's waiting. Besides that Eddie and I would be forever grateful to him for having helped us out and we would be his friends for life. There was no way that Buster would refuse that deal.

We didn't know what the result of the scheme was going to be. But Bruce definitely wouldn't dare go to anyone and squeal on Buster. It'd be too embarrassing for him to do so. Everyone would question Bruce's motive in picking on poor Buster. Maybe we were doing the loner a huge favor since no one had ever paid much attention to him. For the first time in his life, Buster would feel very important.

Bampy's master plan for getting Bruce off my back wasn't exactly one of his all-time favorite schemes.

"Ben," he began, "I want you to realize that what I'm about to recommend to you will seem very different, even crazy. I'm not in love with the idea myself, but I believe it'll work. You're dealing with a bully, right? So my suggestion's not on my list of the top ten problem-solvers. You know that almost all problems aren't dealt with in this tough way. This here kid, Bruce, is a menace who can do a lot of serious damage to you or anyone else if you let him get away with this. He's probably a coward, anyway, if you want to know the truth. Most guys like him are, you know that, don't you?"

Before Bampy had told me his strategy for curing that sore at Port school, he elaborated further on a particular event he had experienced in his young life.

"Please understand, Ben, that in order for you to get rid of a bad thing in your life, sometimes you have to go to extreme measures."

"What do you mean?" I said.

"I mean you must truly want to get rid of the problem. You do, don't you?"

"Yes, Bampy."

"Then listen! Think of it as a good device to wipe out what's bothering you. No one's really going to get badly hurt. When I was a real young guy starting out in the meat business with Swift's, there was this fellow, an evil so-and-so, who, according to the other men in the shop, was suspected of robbing several establishments of their rightful share of beef each month. This guy, we didn't know how, was stealing from a lot of people. He was getting in the way of their making the money coming to them. He was in charge of all the distribution of meat in the whole area. Think about it, Ben."

"So what happened?"

"They did to this perpetrator what was coming to him," Bampy opined. "Do you trust me? If you do, you mustn't ever tell a soul what I'm about to tell you. Can you do that? It'll be our little secret forever, okay Ben?"

"Okay," I said.

"Good. This bad guy, this thief, had to be taught a severe lesson so that he'd never again do the awful things he was doing."

"So what happened?" I asked again. "Did the men kill him?"

My grandfather stared at me as if I'd said something wrong. "No, no, Ben. Don't be silly. You never solve a problem that way. What they did was, they hired a couple of thugs who performed their own brand of punishment on the no-good criminal. It could've been done legally, I suppose, but there was no proof anything illegal had been committed. So in the end the victims of this guy's thievery decided to act in their own way. Of course it was wrong, but what he'd done was much worse. You see? These men had been deprived of their livelihood, of putting food on the table for their families. It hadn't done anything to me—I was a new guy in the company. I just knew about it, that's all. I'm telling you this story to help you out. What happened just happened. Sometimes life is tough, Ben. You have to grin and bear it, go with the punches. The hired thugs beat the man up a little and scared him half to death, told him they'd really hurt him bad if he ever did anything with the meat again. Obviously, the poor slob got the message and turned his life around. The problem not only was solved but the guys wronged were given back their share of the beef. The man responsible was beholden to the fellows for what he'd done. The terrible act was never repeated. A wonderful lesson had been learned. Please don't, Ben, ever tell your father this story or about my instructions on how to deal with Bruce. Please. It's very important for both of us. We're buddies, right?"

"Yes, Bampy."

The carrying out of the Bruce-Buster confrontation was successful: Bruce had a noticeable shiner from Buster's well-timed punches. In school the following day Bruce looked downright defeated and, besides, no other injury had occurred. I rationalized that the "mild beating" our nemesis had received was justified. I wasn't going to feel bad about it, not one bit. In fact, I felt great about it, marvelously relieved. I understood, of course, how wrong it was. Yet I applauded the result it'd rendered. Buster was beaming at his accomplishment, plus he'd performed his usual task of pouncing on people. Only this time he'd done something real special and the wide smile on his face was further testament to that. I'd never seen him in such an exuberant mood. Alice, Eddie, and I were happy. Everyone was happy except Bruce. My grandfather had been right all along in his explanation as to why, once in a great while, it was absolutely necessary to resort to such an extreme measure. Bruce's whole demeanor changed; no longer was he strutting about the school with the superiority the students had become accustomed to. His silence was so unusual that the kids just stared at him in disbelief. He told a couple of friends, who spread the word, that he'd received the black eye by bumping his head against a cupboard door at home. Whether or not anybody believed that story was irrelevant. The only thing that mattered was that Bruce was different. Some of the kids told me they thought his explanation was true. As for any continuation of the gossip he'd been spreading, Bruce's innuendoes ceased. Both Alice and I were pleasantly surprised and comforted but Eddie was stunned by what had come over Bruce.

The following Saturday after the Bruce Hatfield affair I was alone with Alice in her living room. Her mother was upstairs and the record player was on full blast. The song forever remained a soft, blurred sound. Suddenly I kissed her, or maybe she kissed me. I wasn't sure, it happened so fast. I did know one thing, however. That kiss was more life-changing, more exhilarating than the time I got my first base hit for the Little League Athletics. Maybe it was my reward for having done something right for a change. It taught me that oftentimes when I did something for the first time it turned out to be a memorable experience in my life. I lived off that kiss for a long time.

For the first time in my life I'd learned how to deal with adversity. The thing I was the proudest of, however, was that I hadn't run to my father with my problem. Everything would've gone out of kilter if I had. My father and Mr. Hatfield would've gone after each other like two angry dogs. To be honest with myself, I'd solicited the help of my grandfather and then had used Eddie and Buster, not to mention Alice's support, to carry out the plan. So I hadn't really done it all by myself. In fact, I had been a small piece of the scheme. I wasn't as smart as I thought I was. I'd discovered that you always needed others in most situations. It would've been much easier had I initially complained about Bruce to my Dad, yet it would've seemed less challenging for me. I'd chosen a more difficult route and had become more independent as a result.

Perhaps the healthiest aspect of my attending Port School was the distance factor. I was by then used to being away from home. That was extremely beneficial and important. It acted as an ally to my growing up. When I was forced to stand on my own two feet and confront things more directly, I reaped some positive results.

I was anticipating the following year with a newness of spirit and with the hope that I was becoming a more responsible kid. I had a long way to go. Only time would tell how things would develop in the near future.

CHAPTER TWENTY-ONE

The arrival of Dr. Vincent Battaglio on the educational scene in Danvers was a heralded event. Practically everyone was talking about him. He was only twenty-seven and had already attained the position of Assistant Principal at Holten-Richmond Junior High School. It was announced that the following year, when I'd be a sixth-grader, he was going to be the new principal of Port School. Dr. Battaglio was the youngest person to ever reach that plateau in the state of Massachusetts. More importantly, however, was the news that he was an avid baseball buff. One of his goals was to help some of the Port kids develop a good team representing the school. There were only two teams in the elementary system in Danvers, the other one coming from the larger section of Tapleyville. The "wharf rats" annually clashed with "the villagers." Boys in both the fifth and sixth grades were to be included whereby Port and Tapleyville tried to field the best nine guys available in their respective schools. They played each other only once each spring. It was a big deal for each school because it served the duel purposes of healthy competition and acquiring sole bragging rights. It generated a lot of excitement, so much so that all the students were abuzz over it.

Dr. Battaglio was enthused over the challenge of developing a formidable group of guys to face the villagers. It wasn't as if he'd be out there each day to instruct us in the finer points of the sport. He simply didn't have the time to spare for that. We had to practice on our own in the dirt yard of the school or at home in our spare time. A couple of days before the big game he was going to get together with the team to discuss whatever strategy was necessary. All the kids were going to be given an equal chance. The important decisions that had to be made centered on the players and what positions they'd play. The best possible lineup had to be decided. Who was going to be the pitcher and catcher, the clean-up hitter?

Dr. Battaglio's knowledge of the potential players at Port School had to come from general hearsay and reports about each kid interested in participating. This wasn't an organized event as if we were in the Danvers Little League. It was an easy way to bring two groups of enthusiastic kids together who wanted the thrill of competing against each other. Furthermore, it was my first opportunity of playing on a team that didn't include Scott; I was going to be on my own.

Dr. Battaglio had to juggle his time between the two schools. He began coming to Port School in early April because he wanted to familiarize himself with all the Port kids he'd be supervising the following year. He also wished to get a general idea about the ability of our players. I didn't know why but he inquired about me. He'd heard things. He knew about the East Danvers Red Sox; we'd been kind of famous in the town.

In the second week of May the man who'd be my new principal the following fall approached me at lunchtime outside in the hall.

"Hi, you're Ben Robblee, right? How are you?" he asked, shaking my hand. "I'd like to talk with you. Have you got a few moments?"

I shook my head and said, "Yes, you're the new Assistant Principal at Holten- Richmond Junior High, aren't you?"

"That's right, Ben. I'm Dr. Battaglio. I guess things get around quickly in Danvers, don't they?"

"What do you want to talk to me about?" I inquired, a little bit nervous.

"Well, you probably have heard I'll be coaching you pretty soon when you guys play at Tapleyville, so I came here to ask you if you'd like to pitch for the team?"

I was taken aback but answered, "Gee, Dr. Battaglio, I don't know. Danny Doheney is a great pitcher—he's the kid to talk to. I'm not as good as he is. I only did a little pitching for the East Danvers Red Sox. Danny's the star."

"Yes, I've heard about Danny, but he told me yesterday that he didn't want to play for the Port team. He's sick of baseball, apparently. He was real nice about it, yet he simply isn't interested right now. Maybe he'll want to play again in high school."

"Oh," I said, feeling a little disappointed. "Like I told

you, I'm really not a regular pitcher. I did hurl a few innings in relief when our team was way ahead, but that's different from being a starter."

"Will you at least consider it, Ben?"

"Sure, I can try it, I suppose. I can play any position except catcher."

"Fine, Ben, we'll leave it at that. Let's just wait and see. Think about it, I believe strongly you'd do well on the mound. I'll be around next week, tell me then. Sleep on it. It's not the end of the world. I want you to do whatever you want."

As soon as school let out that day I went running to Danny.

"What's this I hear from Dr. Battaglio that you don't want to pitch for the Port team, Danny?" I remarked, concerned over my ex-teammate's refusal to play.

Danny was wearing a Red Sox jacket and also had on a St. Louis Cardinals cap. He seemed much taller than when he'd attended Williams School the previous year. Also, there was a remarkable transformation in his attitude that surprised me. I didn't know exactly what it was but I didn't like it.

He flinched at me and declared, "Why should I pitch for the crummy Port team? I'm too good for them," he boasted, his big front teeth flashing. "I don't have time to pitch for a group of cruddy players. Someday, Ben, I'm going to be in the National League." He kept taking his Cardinals cap on and off and staring at it. "My father says I'd be wasting my time with you guys. Remember when I didn't make the

Danvers Little League All-Star Team? Dad was so mad he wanted to kill the people who made up that team. And I agreed with him. I was the best pitcher in the whole league. You know that, don't you? Admit it, Ben."

I smiled at him and said, "Yes, Danny, you were the best hurler in the league. I remember your father asking me at the Beverly-Danvers All-Star game, you know, the day it started to pour out in the sixth inning, ending the battle at 8-8. That was the game where I slipped in right field going after a fly ball and two runs came in for Beverly. Boy, I felt real bad about that. When I asked Coach Davis about it later on, he made me feel much better. 'Don't worry, Ben, anyone can trip in the rain. It wasn't even an error.' I'll never forget that play."

"I remember that game, Ben. I was there and, believe me, I felt awful for you. You've always been a good guy. But Scott is a real pain in the neck. I'm fed up to here with Scott ordering us around like we're babies. Does he think he's God? He isn't, you know." Danny gave such an obscene gesture, so unusual for him, that his mother would've squelched him had she been there.

"So when do you think you'll play baseball again?" I said.

"I don't know, maybe never. No, I think maybe in high school. Who knows? Someday I'm going to be a big star for the Cardinals or Dodgers. Then those guys who didn't choose me for the all-star team can go you-know-where."

I stood there looking at Danny, a little confused. On

the one hand I didn't like his bravado but, on the other, I admired it.

"Ben, someday I'm going to be another Bobby Shantz or Mel Parnell. They're great southpaws. Everyone will beg for my autograph, you wait and see. Don't worry, I'll be glad to give you one." Danny began to laugh out loud.

"Oh, thanks, Danny."

Shortly thereafter the bus came from Danvers Square to pick us up for the short ride home.

Dr. Battaglio talked me into pitching against the Tapleyville nine. The game was for all the marbles. Each school had some good ballplayers and some who were mediocre. I was a little shaky over being designated as the main guy on the mound. Even though I wasn't a star performer I guessed that the decision to have me pitch put me a notch above average. Because I had an older brother that always stood out as a star in everyone's eyes, there was no possible way I'd ever classify myself that highly. Maybe that was the reason I wanted to be judged on my own merits. I was well aware of the fact that if Danny had wanted to pitch that game I never would've been in that position to begin with. That gave me great incentive to prove to myself and to others that I was able to get the job done.

The contest with Tapleyville occurred in the third week of May. The weather had calmed down after several weeks of rain and colder-than-usual temperatures. Three-thirty was the starting time. Dr. Battaglio made it appear as if it were an extravaganza. He managed to have all the guys pumped up. It was a sunny day without a cloud in the sky. Several girls from Port School congregated behind our splintery bench. Alice was there, which made me beam with pride. I was so glad! Everyone kept yelling encouraging words to us. Dr. Battaglio kept studying me as I warmed up before the game. My arm felt great. Having played games as a member of the East Danvers Red Sox, I should've been confident, but I wasn't. The main reason I was so fidgety was the way the fellow who'd be my future principal was acting. He didn't stop asking me how I felt and if I was ready to pitch the game of my life. Suddenly I assumed the persona of Vic Raschi of the New York Yankees. I was pitching the seventh game of the World Series against the Dodgers. Everything depended on my performance. Was I up to the challenge?

The catcher, a rugged kid named "Moose," kept after me by constantly chatting. "Let's go, Ben, put it in there." I was hoping he'd just shut up for a second. I think he was trying to impress Dr. Battaglio with his superficial display of shouting. "Ben baby, let's see your burner." Then he smacked his fist into his catcher's mitt. "That's it, good pitch." I needed this distraction about as much as I needed the awful-tasting cough medicine my mother always gave me when I had a bad cold.

The game produced a lot of runs with us on the winning end of an 11-5 score. It went the usual seven innings. I managed to go the distance. I gave up eight hits, one of them a homerun, four walks, and I fanned ten batters. That wasn't a bad effort on my part. I was pleased with my overall performance. The most important thing was that we'd won. And I smacked a double and a single in five trips to the plate. I hit second in the lineup. I didn't realize it until a few days later but my reputation shot up several points among the students at Port School. For a week or so I actually considered myself a budding star. At times I felt great about my achievement and Alice certainly was happy for me. Now I knew what Scott always went through when he pitched, but I wasn't sure I liked it. It was a feeling I wasn't used to. The unfortunate thing, however, was that I'd never informed Dad about the game. I wondered what he would've thought of my performance that afternoon.

The humorous aspect to our decisive victory over Tapleyville was that I was now a member of a team labeled as "the bad guys." I was a Port kid in the eyes of all the Tapleyville players. They were "the good guys." For some reason, I loved being a bad guy! The moment I became aware that I was on the winning team was an exciting one in my life. I savored every second and wanted desperately to hang onto that feeling forever. That's what it meant to be a kid growing up in Danvers during those innocent days in the fifth grade. I fully enjoyed them while they lasted.

The only down side to the game was the way Dr. Battaglio carried on. He scrutinized every single pitch I threw. It was uncomfortable being under the microscope.

He paced back-and-forth from behind our bench to the backstop where a tall screen prevented past balls and foul tips from going beyond a certain point. A few times I tried to impress him by zinging in the ball to Moose and it ended up being a wild pitch. Once I even hit one of their batters. I tried not to think about it, but it was difficult.

After each inning while I was sitting on the bench, Dr. Battaglio came over to me to offer some advice. I figured he thought he was Casey Stengel or something. At first I felt pressured from his presence. After two or three innings, though, I pretended I was heeding his every word by shaking my head. It worked. I did appreciate what he was trying to accomplish. But he was giving me all his attention and avoiding the rest of the team. It made me feel awkward in front of them. I'd always been just one of the regular players on the East Danvers Red Sox. It forced me to try harder, but I wasn't used to it.

The remainder of my fifth-grade year at Port School completed one of the happiest times of my life. During the last two months in school I cherished the kudos I received for my accomplishment on the field of play. But that paled to my having met the sweetest girl in the world and a friend, albeit a buffoon, who always stood by my side. Alice and Eddie were ingrained in my memory. And there hadn't been the emotional presence of either my father or Scott to get in my way. The important thing was that I had stood proudly with my friends; my father's discipline and the weight of my brother's athletic prowess weren't around to sap my confidence. I was slowly growing up and learning to adapt.

My baseball career, however short it was, always seemed promising and it was the only sport I actually enjoyed playing at times. My participation in athletics ended abruptly on that fateful, chilly Friday night of October 12th in my senior year of high school during a football game under the lights.

My baseball coach in high school didn't want to use me. I did mind terribly not being included on the varsity baseball team. I became depressed over it. After all, in junior high I played left field and second base for the freshman nine that went an amazing eleven wins and one defeat, a great record. A strong Polish kid named Stan Rochenski pitched nine of those eleven victories for our team. My average was .324, 11 hits in 34 trips to the plate, not bad in my opinion. I was the left fielder for the champion YMCA club in the Pony League, the best outfit I ever played for. We won out over a great CYO team in the championship series, three games to none (Scott was the superstar, winning nine regular season games on the mound as well as two in the playoffs). Four members of that YMCA nine went on to stardom in high school and college. They were absolutely spectacular. Just being a part of that team was a wonderful experience, something for me to be proud of. I also played for Ferncroft from the old Twilight League for two summers during my sophomore and junior years in high school. My batting average slipped to .278 and .250, pretty good considering I was playing against some guys much older than I was. So when the high school baseball coach neglected me, I was livid over it. My self-esteem dropped to an all-time low. I thought of myself as below average. My status those two crummy years stood firmly as a member of the junior-varsity team. I never forgot that on one particular afternoon, when the coach had me scheduled to bat fourth, I decided to skip the stupid game entirely and instead went home to watch American Bandstand. I looked upon myself as a true rebel during those few hours and figured that, just maybe, the coach would kick me off the team. I was dead wrong. He never even mentioned my absence the following day. That's how much he cared. By then my interest level had fallen to zero. I knew I was good enough to play for the first team and when I didn't my opinion of myself dropped to an all-time low. No matter how hard I plugged away and tried to impress the coach, the more I didn't have a prayer of playing. Though it was my decision to stay on the team, I should've handed in my uniform and quit—but I didn't.

CHAPTER TWENTY-TWO

The one constant I learned throughout my school years was that nothing was constant. My Port School stay gave me an opportunity to break away from the emotional confines of my home. I loved being in my house, perhaps too much. I was always comfortable being by myself. By going from Williams School to Port School I was blatantly introduced to a different world. I had to pass through a labyrinth of both pleasant and unpleasant experiences without the near-by aid of my parents. I discovered, sometimes harshly, that as I entered through each new phase of my life with a certain amount of trepidation, there was always some pain involved. The positive and the negative were forever colliding. However, there wasn't anything I'd experienced in elementary school or junior high that had prepared me in the slightest for what was ahead for me in high school. Nothing could've prepared me for it.

From the moment I began junior high school, all the way through four years of high school, the most dominant force in my life was the sport of football. Not only did I hate it with all the passion that I possessed, but I also wasn't that good at it. I never understood as hard as I tried to how something I didn't even want to participate in was the focus of my existence. Ever since I was a kid going to Williams School, all I'd heard about concerning the awful subject of football was my Uncle "Artie" Foster. He was my grandfather's oldest son and my mother's brother. I secretly called him "Bampy's boy." If anyone familiar with sports were to compare him to anyone in the Robblee family, that person would say he'd been another Scott, Jr. Or rather he'd remark that Scott, Jr. was a replica of Uncle Artie. And just as my brother Scott had a younger brother named Ben, Artie Foster also had a younger brother, my Uncle "Bennie." I had been named after him, which I considered to be a strange coincidence. It was as if the good Lord had cloned, in the same immediate family, two sets of brothers whose characteristics and lives coincided perfectly. Two genuine studs in sports, always in the spotlight, erased whatever exploits their younger brothers were trying to achieve. It was a hopeless spot to be put in. The footnote to this was telling. Life passed us by as we were looking up to our older brothers. As I got older my Uncle Bennie, several years after I got badly hurt, told me to forget about Scott's achievements and to focus on myself. He said that it wasn't worth all that wasted energy to make comparisons. It was excellent advice that I had to follow if I ever wanted to be my own person. Unfortunately Bennie Foster had experienced much tougher times than even I had. There was no doubt about that.

CHAPTER TWENTY-THREE

My introduction to football had come at the age of six or seven. My father and mother had just returned from the Army-Navy classic in Philadelphia in the mid-40s. They both were excited over it, which, in turn, made me interested. That was when Army had a great team with Doc Blanchard and Glenn Davis in the backfield. That duo's picture was all over the covers of national and sport magazines. They were called the "touchdown twins," Mr. Inside and Mr. Outside. I wasn't sure but I thought it was at the tail end of World War II.

A short time after that my Dad bought the three of us kids a new football and some colorful helmets to put on whenever we felt like playing around outdoors on the lawn. Of course we made a big deal out of wearing them, even though Andy's helmet came down to his mouth. He was only two or three years old at the time.

I distinctly recalled one of the helmets: it was dark green with a black stripe over the top of it. It even had a special smell to it. After Scott, Andy, and I had carefully examined each helmet to determine which one we wanted, I insisted on having the green one. Scott wanted the bright red helmet that didn't have any stripe on it. Andy didn't really care which one was his. So we gave him the dark brown helmet with the yellow stripe. He had trouble lifting the stupid thing.

For a week or so I was happy with my green helmet. The odd thing was, though, after continually looking at Andy's brown-and-yellow helmet, I decided I wanted that one for my own because I liked the colors. Andy never wore it anyway because he was unable to see with it on. We switched and that was that.

Occasionally in the fall, as the weather became colder and we no longer even thought about baseball, a group of us boys in the neighborhood got together to play some football. It was nothing serious. It wasn't as if anyone had to look forward to being on the receiving end of a big hit. The East Danvers kids, for the most part, loved baseball much more.

I listened to several football games on the radio. On New Year's Day in 1948 I remembered getting excited over the Michigan-USC game in the Rose Bowl. It wasn't even close. I became a Wolverine fan on that afternoon when Michigan slaughtered the Trojans, 49-0. The more touchdowns they scored the more excited I got. But that was the extent of my interest in football: I only enjoyed it from a distance.

My father often took Scott and me (Andy was too young) to some of the key high school games in the area, especially the Danvers, Beverly, and Salem games. I was just a small kid but I enjoyed looking at the bigger and older players go at it. They seemed like men to me. The one game that stuck out in my mind, however, took place on a cold Saturday afternoon in Lowell, Massachusetts. It was tabbed as the most important game in the state that day. To the eventual winner went the title of Class A Champion in all likelihood. Lowell hadn't lost in over twenty-five games and was considered a slight favorite, notwithstanding the fact that Haverhill also had a potent team. Since I always rooted for the underdog, I was pulling for Haverhill. Plus I liked the colors of their uniforms. They were brown and yellow, just like the helmet I'd snatched from Andy years before. Anyway, in a nip-and-tuck contest between the two powerhouses, the Haverhill "HILLIES" upset the Lowell "RED RAIDERS" by the score of 12-7. There was pandemonium after the game. We were lucky we got out of there alive. The reason I remembered it so well was that the quarterback that afternoon for Haverhill, a kid named Don, was a big star in the contest. He ended up playing at Notre Dame. And Lowell had a huge tackle who was 6'-5" and weighed over two hundred forty pounds. Back then it seemed as if I were watching a giant smash opponents right in front of me. That whole afternoon was amazing.

My first physical experience in football came in the seventh grade. It was the direct result of my father's being a football player in both high school and college. I never heard the end of it. Weighing in at well over two hundred pounds, Dad also was a champion wrestler in the heavyweight division at Allegheny College. His peers affectionately referred to him as "the bruiser." I tried not to care. As a kid, I'd seen a picture of Dad and his Salem High buddy frolicking on the sand at Revere Beach. They were flexing their muscles for the camera. I thought, as I gazed at the two of them in the photo, "big deal."

I went out for football in the seventh grade because either my father wanted me to or I thought he wanted me to. Everything I did in sports was directly connected to him. The lone explanation for this was fear. It was a paralyzing scenario for me, the reason being I only wanted to please him. I wasn't even aware of my own welfare. I was afraid to tell Dad that I didn't want to play. I had visions of myself lying dead on the field after being clobbered by some tough tackler. My father's concern, at my wake, would've centered on the fact that at least I'd given it the old college try. His son was no quitter—that was the most important thing of all to him.

My first game for the Holten-Richmond Junior High School was, ironically, a fairly positive experience for me. I was in awe of how well everything actually went. Our opponent, Swampscott, was a team that almost always produced a winner. That was, to be sure, only a contest between seventh-grade teams. There more than likely weren't going to be any bruisers present to knock me silly. I'd be fibbing if I didn't admit I was very scared. As the opposing team kicked off, signaling the start of the game, that's when the butterflies really became apparent. I was petrified. On the next play I nervously trotted onto the field to start at left halfback on the first offensive series. The game was being played in the outfield of the old Holten High School baseball field. There weren't any white chalk lines drawn to enable anyone to see where we were on the playing surface. The two referees had to guess the yardage gained or lost during each play. Several excited teachers and girls were in attendance to support us. A crowd of about fifty people, some of them parents of the players, attended. All the fans stood on either sideline. Even my father was there, which made me very anxious. The most disappointing thing of all, however, was the fact that Alice, my sweet blonde friend at the Port School, wasn't present to see me play my first organized game of football. I was so aware of this that several times I gazed over at the sidelines expecting to see her cheering me on—but she was not there! Her parents had insisted that she attend a top Catholic school in order to get a better education. Despite the fact that Alice had promised me that she'd always keep in touch, I simply didn't understand and felt somewhat betrayed when I didn't see her at the game.

I was chosen to be the first one to carry the pigskin. Back then we only used the old Princeton single-wing formation, where all four backs were positioned in descending order, like bowling pins, behind the offensive line. The right halfback crouched behind the right end. The quarterback, who called the signals and was the main blocking back, was positioned a little further back behind the right tackle and guard. The fullback was even further back behind the center and was the one who always handed off to the right halfback whenever he was to run with the ball. The left halfback was the deep back to the fullback's left. The football was centered to the fullback or left halfback. I was the left halfback.

On the very first play, the ball was centered to me. It was the 42-hike. I took the football and rambled down the right sideline for about forty yards. Forty yards. It wasn't bad for a kid who didn't think he had it in him. If their safety hadn't knocked me out-of-bounds, I would've scampered for a long touchdown on my first attempt at ever carrying the ball. The blocking on the play was so perfect that no one but the last guy touched me. I glowed inside. I was another Red Grange. Better still, I was an Uncle Artie Foster in the making! Maybe football was okay, after all. That feeling quickly evaporated the next time I ran with the ball tucked tightly under my right arm. The Swampscott linebacker hit me so hard at the line of scrimmage that he forced me backward and upward. I felt his tackle so much that it was a jolt to my system. In the end we lost to our opponents, 18-6. I wasn't concerned over the outcome because I was thinking about all the homework that I had to do that night. My mind hadn't been totally on the contest.

My first game was over. Outside of that one outstanding scamper, I'd performed so-so. I carried the ball about eight times and on half of those runs I was hit real hard. I'd been awakened to the physical aspect of football. I wasn't looking forward to my future on the gridiron.

My eighth-grade and freshman years were about the same as my seventh-grade year had been. I wasn't happy, that was about it. Nothing really super in the way of accomplishments on the football field materialized. Our team was mediocre and I was mediocre. We won a few games. We lost a lot of games. I did make a few nice runs and scored a couple of touchdowns but most of the time I simply stunk. I wasn't into it. By all accounts I was an average athlete. Nothing spectacular would ever come of my playing football. I had an I-don't-care attitude. I wasn't a star and never would be. But since I didn't enjoy the sport at all, it really didn't bother me. It was no big deal. I just wanted to have some fun in whatever I was doing in school or at home. I was the most contented when I was studying, playing my own games, or just thinking. Little did I know that, just ahead, for the next three years of high school, my whole life would be turned inside out and upside down because of the idiotic game of football.

CHAPTER TWENTY-FOUR

I hadn't been on the Holten High School football team for one full practice before I realized what I was facing. I knew it was going to be one of the most difficult struggles of my life. Nothing good would ever come of it. I tried to think positively about it but just couldn't. I thought about Uncle Artie and all those stories. It was the beginning of a three-year experience that would make me miserable for many, many years to come. If I'd been a spunky kid and shown a smidgen of assertiveness at all, I'd have quit immediately, right then and there. That single act would've saved me from years of anguish and pain. I knew that if I chose not to play the guys on the team would've never treated me the same. My popularity would've suffered. But there was really no point whatsoever in my sticking it out to prove to myself or to others that I could do well in football. If I hated doing it so much, why didn't I simply stop doing it? But I didn't stop, and I was angry with myself.

I approached my father that first evening, hoping to let him know how I truly felt about things. I wanted like nothing else to tell him that I wasn't interested anymore in playing football. I practiced over and over again the words

I'd use, but when the time came, I couldn't express my exact feelings. I chickened out—I just couldn't go through with it. He would've looked at me, put his arm around my shoulder, and calmly stated that no son of his was a quitter. He never would've entertained the idea of my not playing on the team. If Scott could do it, so could I! I considered running to my grandfather with the problem but in that particular case it would've been a total waste of time. So in the end I had only myself to blame for not trying to reverse my situation.

There were two things I feared might happen if I continued playing football in high school. I was an excellent student who was conscientious. I was afraid my marks would slip considerably if I didn't concentrate on my subjects. Football would take up the majority of my time and energy. The other factor was my physical health. I constantly worried about getting hurt; I had a premonition of medics carrying me off the field on a stretcher.

The coach was tough: he had the personality of a drill sergeant. I knew he wasn't going to help my situation at all. He was the perfect example of what a football coach shouldn't be. He was too gruff and didn't seem to be aware that I was on the team. Since I wasn't one of "his boys," I was wasting my time. I felt as if I'd be nothing more than one of the tackling dummies used in practice.

In some cases there were guys who played regularly who weren't as capable as a few of the substitutes. That probably happened in every school. It really didn't bother me. I had no desire to play, anyway. The coach was actually doing me a favor. Perhaps the main reason he chose not to put me in a game was because of my brother. Scott had transferred to a well-known prep school, thus depriving the team of a star halfback. There was no doubt Scott would've been the best back on the squad had he stayed to play in Danvers. I didn't think I was treated with the same respect as Scott was. Then again, maybe the coach decided not to play me because of my lack of ability. I never was sure of anything concerning the rotten game of football.

I basically sat on the bench my entire sophomore and junior years. What a colossal waste of time! The coach, surprisingly, managed to put me in a game for a few defensive plays whenever we were way ahead, which was almost never. I didn't play any offense. My bitterness, however, didn't revolve around my not playing but centered, instead, on the precious time I was losing. I didn't study as much as I wanted to. I saw my friends less and less as the season progressed. Because Eddie Howard was in the non-college classes at the high school and had a part-time job, I rarely ran into him. It was as if he no longer existed. That meant that both Alice and Eddie had disappeared altogether from my life. I was lonely. However, during the year when the football season was over, I used to rush home after school at two-thirty in order to catch American Bandstand with Dick Clark on television. I considered myself a great dancer who was a rock-and-roll freak. But most of all I had an unbelievable crush on one of the girls on Bandstand. Her name was Patty and she had black curly hair and a contagious smile.

It went without saying that she was Italian. I even wrote her a letter one day but she never responded. She reminded me of Joey Buccella's sister, Marie. I always wondered how Marie looked later on in life. I'd probably never know but I bet she became a gorgeous young woman. Had she stopped talking so much? If she had, there was some lucky guy way out there in New Mexico who was very contented.

CHAPTER TWENTY-FIVE

My final year in high school was both a pivotal and terrible time for me: it was physically and emotionally jolting. My football injury, I firmly came to believe, interrupted all of my dreams and goals. For me to overcome something of its stature was a grueling task that would last a lifetime. There was, however, one certainty that ruled my every action and thought. Whatever I'd do in the future depended on my working at it a lot harder and accepting the fact that there was going to be a few things I'd never be able to do. It was that simple and it was that complicated.

I felt sorry for myself and was very bitter. Schoolmates found me almost impossible to deal with between classes. I blamed my father. I blamed myself. I blamed the school. There was a reason for what had occurred that awful night on October 12, 1956, in that huge stadium in Lynn, Massachusetts. Things like that just didn't happen; there had be an explanation. Maybe God was against me. Maybe I deserved it. Maybe I was being punished for something I'd done or said. My mother unwittingly added to the confusion by telling all her friends that I was different, that I would never be the same person she'd raised. I was a stranger to her. I could tell she was heartbroken.

As far as my dad was concerned, he didn't seem to possess the slightest clue as to the ramifications that sudden change in my life meant. He didn't seem to care, or so I thought. "I got banged up much worse than that, Ben," he pointed out. "You have to pick yourself up and forget it." That didn't mean he was a bad person. The fact that I'd always had mixed feelings about him and he probably knew it exacerbated the problem. It wasn't going to be easy. I'd have to accept things whether I wanted to or not—if I ever wanted to lick it and get better. It took me a long time, years in fact, before things became unscrambled.

About two months after the actual neck-head injury had taken place, I was admitted unceremoniously to a major hospital in Boston, where I was to stay for two weeks for tests and general observation. My behavior in school had become such that some of the teachers acted differently toward me, treated me as if I were heading toward something serious, even dangerous. "How do you feel today, Ben?" the American History teacher, Mr. Cuddihy, asked me point blank each morning in front of the whole class. That daily ritual started right after I'd returned to school from sick leave. By then everyone was staring at me, or I thought they were. Perhaps I was paranoid. There was only one student, Jimmy Timmerman, a quiet kid who was brilliant in all subjects, who had the insight to realize my predicament. "Don't let this get to you, Ben," he said. Jimmy was forever trying to console me. And since I seldom ran into Eddie Howard anymore, he certainly didn't intercede on my behalf.

I honestly didn't think he was capable of helping me, anyway, because he was probably the same happy-go-lucky kid I'd known at Port School.

That hospital stay was a lonely, mentally challenging period in my young life. A white-haired gentleman, Dr. Goodman, a psychiatrist, was brought in on my case. He appeared to me to be the most unemotional person I'd ever met. I believed if bombs had been exploding all around him, he simply would've turned the other way and ignored the situation at hand. He was that detached. His round, pale face and stiff manner gave out a mysterious aura. The only thing I liked about him was the way his tie contrasted dramatically with his dull blue suit: it was full of bright colors depicting strange-looking flowers. And he continuously was rubbing his chin with his plump fingers.

"So, what's going on with you, Ben?" Dr. Goodman began, tapping on the desk with a pen. "I see that you got hurt in football. How're you feeling?"

"I get a lot of headaches, doctor. Sometimes they're worse than at other times. And I'm always tired."

"I see. That's not good, is it? What brings them on? Have you been thinking about something bad in your life?"

"I think a lot about my accident in football. I don't think it was right. It wasn't fair. I think the coach was dead wrong to keep playing me both ways on offense and defense when I hated it so much. I never should've been hurt. Never!" I emphasized, beginning to sob. "I hate my father and the stupid coach for making me play the stupid game of football. I hate them!"

"Why did they make you play? Didn't you let them know your feelings?"

"I couldn't really tell my father. I tried—but just couldn't, that's all."

"Yes. I see what you were up against. You felt you didn't have anywhere to turn, right? That was quite a pickle you were in."

I didn't say anything because I was too upset.

"Listen to me. You're a good kid. You mustn't allow this to get to you. You've suffered a lot. I understand that. Think of it this way. You could've been crippled for life, am I right? But the most important thing of all is that no one, and I mean absolutely no one, can feel your pain, what you're feeling inside. Only you can. Do you understand what I'm saying?"

"Does that mean that nobody cares about me?"

"Of course they care. I'm sure your parents are very worried about you. But all I'm saying is that they really don't know what you're going through inside."

"I think Mom really cares a lot, doctor. I don't know about Dad."

"Your father perhaps is different than your mother. Don't forget he's a man. He probably doesn't show his feelings as much as your mother does."

"Yes, but she didn't make me play football—he did."

Dr. Goodman rubbed his chin and said, "Yes, maybe that's true. But he wanted you to be like him."

"I don't understand. I don't want to be like Dad! He always makes me do crap around the house just to get me mad."

The doctor hesitated and then declared, "You're no different than most kids. Almost all kids have to do things around the house."

"Yes, but their fathers aren't mean to them."

"Sure, some are. You mustn't always think that he's picking on you, you know."

"What am I supposed to do? Just sit there and let him do it?"

"No, no. Look at me. Fight back! Tell your dad what you're thinking. What's he supposed to do, read your mind?"

"He'll clobber me if I tell him what I think."

"But hasn't he already clobbered you? Think. You're smart. I heard you're a bright kid. You have nothing to lose at this stage in your life. You've already been hurt in football. You're going to find out soon enough that you have to stand up for your rights. No one's going to do that for you."

"Yes, I think I see, doctor."

"And, for goodness sake, stop blaming the coach or your father or anyone else in this world for what happened to you. It's done, you have to pick up the pieces and do it for yourself. Your parents won't always be there to help you, you know."

"If it weren't for him, I never would've been hurt."

"Maybe that's so. But you were hurt and as a result you get headaches and a lot of other terrible things. I do understand, believe me. You still can't hold it against your father forever. I'm sure he's upset over this, too. Maybe that's why he doesn't say anything about it. Not everyone is the same, you know."

"Oh."

"I was speaking with your mother yesterday. She's a fine woman, Ben, a lot like you—but I think she's babying the daylights out of you. Don't get mad but I really think she's too easy on you. It's time for you to grow up a little, don't you think?" Dr. Goodman managed a slight smile. "But the most important thing for you to do now is to snap out of this. Start living a little and accept what happened in that game. It's over and you must deal with it. When you wake up tomorrow morning, say to yourself, 'Today I'm going to start being happy.' Can you do that?" Dr. Goodman stared directly at me.

I sat there looking at the doctor and answered, "I think so—I'll try."

"Good," he said. "That's a good start."

"But I still get angry toward my father for what he did."

"Yes, your father makes mistakes—we all do. He's not God, you know. And your mother does, too. And you do. Unfortunately, nobody's perfect, am I right?"

"Yes, doctor."

"That doesn't mean you have to make excuses for your father or anyone else in your life. He's goofed where you're concerned, I'm sure. Get angry about it—even tell him.

Believe me, he'll think better of you for it."

"He will?" I finally smiled. "That's going to be real difficult."

"One more point," he said, getting up and walking over to me.

"What?"

"Your father also has done a lot of wonderful things for you, hasn't he?"

"Yes," I said softly, almost breaking down.

When I was finished with that fifty-minute session I left feeling a little bit better. I didn't understand everything Dr. Goodman had said to me but I did know something for sure. One thing he had stressed stood out in my mind: I had to snap out of what was eating away at me; if I didn't, it would ultimately ruin my life.

CHAPTER TWENTY-SIX

All during my senior year at Holten High School it was as if someone had forcibly put me on a roller coaster and locked me in the seat and the frightful ride would never stop. I never considered myself important in the general scheme of things because I was simply following orders. I was drifting toward nowhere. In September my only aim was to survive the football season. In the back of my mind there always was the fear of getting hurt. A frail-looking kid whom I'd once casually met at a country club in Wenham and who'd played for a nearby Catholic school had died of a neck injury in a game the year before. His untimely death had lingered in the minds of many, including myself. Life was precious and I felt I shouldn't be playing around with it. That was precisely why I wanted to do those things I loved doing. But I knew it was impossible.

There was a new football coach in town. My former coach had been promoted to Athletic Director. At first I was relieved. The new man, probably in his mid-fifties, had a brusque manner about him; he was an old-timer as far as coaching went, in the twilight of his career. As fate would have it, he was also a close friend of my father's and was well known for having been an outstanding athlete at Boston University and a winning coach in Salem. Amazingly he'd been the young basketball coach at Salem High School when Dad had quit the team. What an incredible development! Besides that he was familiar with my Uncle Artie's football exploits. I knew I was sunk. Immediately, without my having done anything, I was forced into harm's way. There was no doubt as to my future status on the team. If I didn't end up as a starter, I was surely going to be a regular performer. "Coach," as I always called him to his face once I'd met him and Dad had great things in store for me. In those days we didn't start practicing until the beginning of school. Several of the more fanatical players usually got together during the summer to practice without any supervision. Not me, however.

The first week of school I detected Coach walking around the high school lobbying for prospective candidates. He was trying to coax some of the bigger boys into playing. I conveniently stayed out of sight because I wanted no part of it. It was announced that the following day he'd be conducting sign-up sessions right after school. Kids interested in going out for the team were encouraged to do so by reporting to the cafeteria. Coach wanted to speak to each guy individually.

The first two days we were supposed to report I did something even I didn't think I'd ever have the guts to do. I went right home after school to do my homework and to watch American Bandstand. It gave me another chance to see Patty dance.

That was the way it went for two days. I was obviously stalling for time and I was curious, while I was dillydallying around like that, as to what Coach was thinking about my not reporting. Maybe he hadn't even noticed. But deep down I doubted that.

During that second evening, when my father approached me, I knew something was up.

"Ben, have you signed up for football yet?" He seemed quite concerned as he looked directly at me. "I was talking with the coach today and he said he hadn't seen you at all."

For a few seconds I said nothing, but then replied, "No, Dad, I haven't signed up. I'm not sure I want to."

"What! That's nonsense, Ben. Of course you want to. Don't be silly. This is a great opportunity for you. Don't you see? You have a new coach who'll give you a big chance to shine. And he's real fair, too. You won't have to worry anymore like you did the past two seasons about sitting on the bench."

"I don't really care about playing, Dad. Please," I begged, "don't make me."

"I won't hear of it, Ben! I've already told him you're ready to show him what you can do. Once you get going, you'll see how much fun it'll be. After all, Scott did well—you can, too. You might turn out to be even better than your brother. You'll never know if you don't try."

I felt sick and defeated inside. I fumbled and blurted

out, "I don't know, Dad."

"Well, I know! Don't disappoint me. You're going out for football and that's that. I won't take no for an answer. No son of mine is a quitter. I went through the whole process and you can also. That's the way it's going to be, Ben."

"I suppose you're right, Dad," I said, not really meaning it. I'd given in and I knew instinctively that I didn't have any other choice. It was odd but I was both relieved and disturbed by my response. No longer did I have to do verbal battle with him.

I sealed our deal by faking a conciliatory smile and left the living room for my bedroom, which I occupied all on my own. Scott was playing football at a famous prep school in Massachusetts and I realized I had to do the same at my school. Why hadn't my father even asked me if I wanted to play? I'd never been given a fair chance to express my real opposition. I'd tried but ultimately failed. In my room late that evening I sat on the edge of my bed and was lost in my thoughts. All sorts of emotions that made me more confused surfaced. It was at that very moment I truly understood the doom awaiting me. Was I going to survive?

The next afternoon after classes I forced myself to go to the cafeteria and signed up. Coach was very pleased I'd decided to play. He beamed at me and immediately made a reference to my Uncle Artie and how great he'd been. Artie Foster had been the outstanding high-school back in Massachusetts and at the University of New Hampshire and my father hadn't been any slouch, either. He'd been a fierce tackler in his day. Coach hoped that I possessed some of the qualities of both of them. He'd see me the following Monday for practice. We only had a few weeks before our first game with Newburyport. After talking with him, I went home and pondered my fate. With expectations my father and Coach had put on me, how was I supposed to deal with the pressure? Everything was caving in on me.

That whole weekend I was a wreck. I didn't study much. I didn't say a word to anyone. I had trouble eating.

I had done something demeaning, however, during my third year in high school while involved in a "scrub game." It'd proven the point that I despised football. Anything I could do to wiggle out of my playing was well worth the try. On one particularly tough series of downs, I was hit hard while running around the left end on the 23 Reverse. I didn't see the defensive player coming, so I was temporarily stunned on the play. For a second I didn't know where I was. It was a legitimate tackle, perfectly timed. My neck snapped slightly, causing me some pain. I panicked. Then I went out of control, yelling and pointing toward my neck. My thoughts turned to that poor kid who'd been killed earlier that same year. The coach whom I disliked came running over after being summoned by the assistant coach. He administered to me by calming me down and ordering someone nearby, a man watching the practice, to drive me immediately to the doctor's office up the street from the practice field. I didn't know why but I might've overplayed the incident. There certainly had been a lot of attention paid to me during that moment. The coach treated me with tremendous compassion, of which I was always grateful. He even mentioned to me later on that he knew I'd been thinking about that kid who'd died.

The doctor took a good look at me and said I was fine and gave me permission to play, which disappointed me no end. I had a slightly strained neck and was told not to participate in any contact for several days. That was the extent of the whole thing. My gimmick had produced no result! What then happened astounded me. During the next practice the coach, again showing great empathy, told me that it was obvious to him that I didn't want to play football. Why didn't I just quit? He wasn't ordering me to do so—he was merely suggesting it to me. He hinted that he knew my father wanted me to play, but it wasn't his place to tell Dad that I shouldn't. Why should I stick it out if I didn't want to? I'd never realized up until then how understanding he was.

The football team my senior year at Holten High School was way below average in ability. We won only three of ten games. There was only one spectacular player on the team, that being the Captain, "Hammering Hank," who played offensive end and defensive linebacker. He made a third of all the tackles that fall. Most of the starting eleven guys played both ways. Without our leader Hank we would've gone 0-10. There was no doubt about that.

I never forgot our first game with the Newburyport "Clippers." They were one of the more powerful teams in the area and had produced some famous football players over the years. We were at least a two-touchdown underdog. Coach elected to start Danny Doheney of East Danvers Red Sox fame instead of me at halfback. The only assignment I was given was to receive kickoffs. I wasn't disappointed—if anything, I was glad over this. However, as fate would have it, on the very first play of the game, I received the kickoff on my five and returned it to the thirty, only to fumble the ball. They then went down the field and scored within three minutes. Right off the bat I'd been the heel! As things developed it was the only touchdown of the half. The Clippers eventually won, 19-0. That one stupid return was the only play in which I participated during the entire game. At home that night, Dad grumbled over my lack of playing time.

For the next four games I shared the right halfback position with Danny. We were shuffled in and out after each play. Neither one of us liked that arrangement. Danny had decided, after several years of not pitching at all, that it was time for him to return to baseball during the spring. He turned out to be the best hurler on the high school nine for three seasons. So his decision to forego baseball years before had been a wise one. At least he knew what he'd wanted to do and had proceeded to do it, unlike me. He had a head on his shoulders—I didn't.

Danny and I also played safety on defense and were occasionally called upon to return punts. I remained the main kickoff guy. It wasn't as if we were competing against one another. We really weren't concerned over each other's performance because he wasn't that fond of football, either. We constantly joked over the fact that we were being used as substitutes just like Paul Brown of the old Cleveland Browns used to do with his offensive guards. That proved to me that I was an average player at best. Since my father and Coach were close friends, if I'd had any talent at all I would've been playing much more.

I managed to make one punt return of about forty yards against a mediocre Punchard High eleven. And on another play against a much stronger Woburn team I received a kick-off and ran up the middle of the field for about thirty-five yards before being tackled. On that particular play two of their players collided head-on and had to be assisted off the field.

My father was furious with Coach; Dad's dissatisfaction over my amount of playing time forced him to act. This wasn't to bode well for me. The only reason I knew about that new development was that he told me he'd spoken to Coach about it. That put me in an awkward spot. What was I supposed to think? As far as I was concerned, I was performing much better than expected. I'd made some decent runs and had survived the first five games without a hitch. I had five more to go and I'd never have to worry anymore about football. I compared it to my being in a long battle that was halfway over. Would I be able to escape harm through several more skirmishes? Just the thought of it made me more nervous.

But Dad had to intercede on my behalf. I was told that next day in the locker room that I'd be playing full-time the next game at right halfback and safety. Coach was going to switch Danny Doheney to right end to receive some passes. I didn't believe it! I was boiling inside and full of fear over that new development. I didn't have the confidence that I was capable of playing both ways for forty minutes. I would've accepted playing only right halfback. I didn't accept what was happening to me.

There was an irony connected to that game which didn't escape me. It was to be the only night game on our schedule plus we also were pitted against a strong Catholic team, St. Francis High, who was enjoying its finest season in twenty years. How encouraging, I thought. It wasn't the same school where that boy had been killed, but the mere fact that it was a Catholic team we'd be up against was too coincidental. It just wasn't possible. It was a known fact that parochial schools fielded much stronger teams than public schools did. Another twist of fate was that I'd asked my father after the eighth grade if he'd allow me to attend the Catholic school near our home, the same one where that player's death occurred three years later. However, we were Protestant. I considered that school to be the best one in the area. Dad wouldn't hear of it. If I'd gone there, I never would've played any football because I wouldn't have been good enough.

I was wound up tight for that whole week prior to the game. It was to be played on a Friday night under the lights and was to be heard over the local radio station, WESX. We seldom had our games broadcast, so that gave it a certain amount of drama. Just the thought that a large crowd might be both present and listening in added to my uneasiness. I was wary of making a big mistake. St. Francis was located in the largest city on the North Shore and the field, an old but classic stadium, had been the scene of many historic games. It had cement stairs and seats and looked like a small Roman Coliseum. In the old days of the 30s and 40s perhaps as many as twenty thousand fans had packed the place to watch two powerhouses go at it. The great Harry Agganis had performed brilliantly there. We'd be lucky to have two thousand in attendance. It wasn't a big deal in the eyes of the media. But to the players on both teams it was. Our record was two wins and three losses. Our opponents were undefeated and, barring a miracle, would in all likelihood go through the season unscathed. To be playing full-time against a team of that caliber was more than a challenge. It was synonymous with suicide.

The game fell on October 12th, Columbus Day. Even though it was a holiday, we went to school that day. The year was 1956. It was a clear, crisp night and, as we climbed the steps from under the stadium into the spotlight, I had one of the strangest feelings I'd ever had in my life. The crowd was much larger than expected. It was spooky. I didn't know what to expect. Was I going to do well or was I entering a danger zone out of which I couldn't escape? I didn't want to think about it; I just wanted to focus on the game.

Our opponents wore uniforms that were all yellow. Yellow jerseys with blue numerals and yellow pants with blue stripes. Compared to our colors of royal blue and white they were an ugly sight. But that didn't really matter. They were a great team with speedy backs and a big line. That's all we were concerned about. Uniforms didn't make a team jell. Players did. Their quarterback was the outstanding signal-caller on the North Shore. They also had three linemen that, for those days, were considered huge. For some football players this contest was a dream come true. For me it was a nightmare.

I caught the opening kickoff on about the ten and dashed to the forty-seven yard line. I saw one huge yellow blur coming my way. Then I heard loud cheers coming from the stands. "Ben Robblee on the return," the loudspeaker blared. It was a remarkable effort on my part. My attitude improved on the first play of the game. My brother Andy told me later on that the radio announcer had commented that I should've broken it for a touchdown. I'd had a hole as big as a Mack Truck to run through. What the announcer didn't know was that I hadn't been aware of that. Fear had propelled me to run as if my life depended on it. I had no delusions of grandeur. I simply wanted to do my best and have the game end.

The contest was so one-sided that the outcome was never in doubt. St. Francis had totally dominated us. With three minutes remaining on the scoreboard the score was 33-6. It was embarrassing. Once again Captain Hank, who never disappointed Coach, was the lone standout. I managed to make a few short gains and some tackles on defense. But I didn't perform spectacularly. That run on the opening play had been my highlight of the night. I'd reverted to my natural state of being average, where I belonged.

I'd played admirably considering the strength of St. Francis. We never would've beaten them, anyway. We'd given it everything we had. That was all anyone could expect. With only a little time left why didn't Coach put in the subs to finish out the game? It was over! The winning team had substituted freely to allow everyone to play. There wasn't a sane reason I should've been left in the game.

Besides that, I was exhausted. It was my misfortune that I was ordered to stay put. By the looks of the other players I reasoned that they felt the same.

CHAPTER TWENTY-SEVEN

St. Francis's punter was standing on his own thirty on fourth down. We'd stopped them on their last series. I was very tired and not a little bothered by the fact that I was waiting on my twenty-five yard line to receive the punt. I thought Coach was crazy for making most of the guys who'd been playing the whole game stay in. It made absolutely no sense to me at all. The ball was snapped and the punter sent it high into the night sky. It was a great punt. I looked up to see where it was. There was an obstructive glare emanating from the stadium's lights. The ball was coming directly at me and descended quickly. At the very last moment I saw it and tried to catch it, but I failed to judge the exact location of its landing. I subsequently dropped the ball and it bounced right in front of me. I should've just fallen on it—but I didn't. Instead, I foolishly attempted to pick it up. In the process of retrieving it I kicked it with my right foot—at least that was what some of the players said I did. I wasn't focused on the issue at hand. That failure of mine was the worst mistake I ever made in my life! I didn't know where the stupid ball was! I lost track of the fact that there were several St. Francis players coming ferociously at me and obviously didn't realize how hard a hit they were going to put on me. They'd been trained to beat up the enemy, the players on the opposing team. That's exactly what they proceeded to do. There was a tremendous thud coming from both the top and sides of my helmet. That was all I remembered.

I came to in the visitors' locker room. I felt dizzy and totally disoriented. I didn't know what really had happened. I was stretched out on a table and I noticed there were several people milling about the room, which confused me even more. Hank came up to me and said, "You played a great game, Ben. Don't sweat it, you'll be okay." He touched my bare shoulder and smiled, trying to take my mind off what had just happened to me. He was a welcomed sight and certainly deserved to be our Captain. Some of the other players asked me how I was. I didn't answer them because I didn't really know. Finally, Coach made a brief appearance and said matter-of-factly, "You'll be fine, Ben." Then he abruptly left. My father never showed up.

CHAPTER TWENTY-EIGHT

I never understood or accepted what transpired in the next few weeks. My father and Coach actually believed, after my sitting out one game, that I was ready to play the final three games of the season. That I could, in fact, return in perfect condition. I didn't know what I could've done to dissuade them. I thought the only solution to this impasse was to either run away from home or go to the school authorities to complain. In those days both options were out of the question. The school doctor, Dr. Deerfield, wanting me to call it quits, actually informed Dad that it was unwise for me to continue playing on the team. He said that I was "psychologically unfit" for football (I found out about this much later). To be honest, I straightforwardly informed Dr. Deerfield during my appointment how much I detested the sport. My father, as expected, disagreed (he bawled me out for having told the doctor anything in the first place). The Athletic Director, the coach my sophomore and junior years, agreed flat out that I should "hang it up." It wasn't worth the risk. He didn't want me to get injured again. Besides, I knew we had a crummy team, anyway. Even if I'd been twice the runner I really was, it wouldn't have made any difference.

I felt as if my father's main concern centered on my proving that I was a man instead of on my overall health. His image of himself as a father was more important to him.

Dad didn't entertain the thought of my not playing. What he proceeded to do defied all reason. He went to an old high school teammate of his, Dr. Donaldson in Salem, and had him write up a permission slip allowing me to resume playing football. I didn't learn about this until many years later after my father had died. My first coach, the one I hadn't liked, informed me of what my Dad had done the day before he was to be inducted into the Holten High School Hall Of Fame. I'd called him to congratulate him on his wonderful achievement. It didn't take a genius to imagine how I felt after hearing this news. I was both appalled and disappointed.

Following a week off I started the next game against Swampscott High School, known for their outstanding teams. I wasn't in the proper emotional state to do anything, let alone play more football. I did, nonetheless, carry the ball three times for about fourteen yards in the first quarter. It appeared to me as if all the players on the field were "way out there" and I was "way in here." I simply wasn't focused at all. It was scary: my world was disintegrating.

On the first play of the second quarter the ball was handed to me. I had a huge hole in front of me; I only had to run straight ahead. It was clear sailing all the way. It would've been a touchdown of about seventy yards. But I stopped at the line of scrimmage right before I could've sprinted for a score. I didn't know where I was or what I was doing. I was in a state of panic. Coach stood on the sidelines and yelled viciously at me, making me feel belittled.

The Athletic Director rushed from the sidelines and escorted me off the field of play in front of all the fans. It was difficult for me to walk. My legs were wobbly and I felt deeply embarrassed that I was the center of attention. I wasn't sure of my ex-coach's exact words but I thought they were, "Your playing days are over, my friend." He quickly took me to the locker room and later drove me back to Danvers in his own car. It went without saying that his particular act on my behalf concluded my high school football career. The man had probably saved me from further injury and possible disaster. I was always appreciative of what he'd done for me. The fact that an adult and an authority figure I'd disliked throughout high school had become my savior was an astounding irony.

I felt tremendously relieved, as if no longer would I be forced to play the sport I hated. But it'd taken a lot to prove the point! It was as if someone who knew of my dilemma had unbuckled the seat holding me in the roller coaster and set me free. I was able to breathe after such a long, long time. It didn't seem to bother me anymore what my Dad or Coach thought. They could both go to the devil! The amazing thing was that neither of them ever said another word to me about football. Not one stupid word. At home my father treated me as if nothing unusual had happened. Whenever I ran into Coach he did the same. No reaction. I wasn't surprised at all. I no longer was of any use to them.

CHAPTER TWENTY-NINE

A wonderful surprise occurred many years later. Eddie Howard called me out of nowhere and wanted to know if it were possible for us to get together.

"Oh, Eddie, I can't tell you how happy I am that you got in touch with me. Where have you been all these years, on the comedy circuit?"

He gave out a loud laugh and answered by telling me he'd been living in Peabody, Massachusetts, which bordered Danvers and was known for its many leather factories. "I had to call you, buddy," he said in an anxious tone. "Let's meet some night at Louie's for a pizza. God, I miss the Port so much. I keep telling Nicole we should move back there."

"Sure, that sounds great to me. How's Friday evening?"

"Perfect, I'm not doing nothing, as usual," he cracked. "I'm not exactly a playboy, if you get my drift."

I'd lost contact with Eddie even though we both had attended Holten High School. It was funny, but I'd always seemed to gravitate toward college-bound kids while he, on the other hand, was strictly a "commercial course" guy. Another factor that had played a strong part in our separation was that I was an athlete—he wasn't. Cliques formed and friendships developed according to social status. Did that mean that many students missed out on the possibility of getting to know kids who might've been friends?

Friday evening came way too slowly. I was so unhinged that I almost became ill over the anticipation of seeing Eddie after so long a period. It had been a lifetime. How had he changed and what would his reaction to me be?

I decided to add a little drama to our meeting by entering the rear door of Louie's. I clearly remembered Eddie's description years ago of how he'd rescue his father late at night from Louie's.

My fifth-grade buddy was standing right inside the door. Just a little bit away I was able to hear an incoherent mishmash of male voices. I knew that as soon we entered the inside door to the bar it would be difficult for us to hear one another. We'd have to talk loud.

"Hey, Ben baby, how're you doing, pal?" he half-shouted, gripping my hand like a vise. "Put it there. Let's go inside where the action is. Wait until you taste their pepperoni pizza. It's unreal."

I never told him I'd only gone inside Louie's a couple of times in my life, and that had been through the front door. The image I'd always had of that pizza joint was different from Eddie's. In my mind it was an unsavory place where questionable characters went. If I'd eaten there with Eddie or someone else in the old days, I definitely wouldn't have divulged it to my parents.

Eddie had gotten a lot heavier. His face, very ruddy,

was filled out to such an extent that his eyes seemed to be having a difficult time peeking out from behind the top of his cheeks. He looked much older than I did. But the one thing I noticed the most about him was the texture of his hands. They had the feel of sandpaper and were incredibly strong and smacked of hard work. That handshake of his came close to crushing my hand.

"Let's sit here," he suggested, pointing to two vacant stools on one end of the bar. Two pretty women wearing aqua t-shirts with Louie's imprinted on the front were mixing drinks and handing out Bud beers as if the world would suddenly stop revolving should they stop. The owner, Louie Mazzarini, now in his late sixties, was standing near the female bartenders as the Director of Operations. That had been his whole life. Every now and then a male customer motioned to him, making sure Louie knew he was there. The Red Sox game was on television, causing a lot of loud banter and waving of arms. Whatever passion I'd once had for baseball had waned; no longer was I the least bit interested in any pitching and batting records or what team was leading the league.

"Boy, when I used to come here years ago, the girls were never dressed like this, you know it?"

"Yeah, how were they dressed, Eddie?"

"You know, they wore white shirts that had long sleeves. Remember?"

I shook my head as if to agree and said, "So what's going on with you? You must have tons of information for me."

"You know me, buddy. I'm a regular information center," he joked. "So will it be a beer for you?"

I hesitated and said firmly, "No. I wish I could, but I'm taking some medication for my headaches. You know—don't you?"

"Yeah, I think I remember. I almost forgot, you were hurt in football, weren't you?"

"It seems that everywhere I go in Danvers, that's what people remind me of. Even now for Godsake. When will it stop?"

"What do you want to drink, my treat. We'll get a large pepperoni, okay?"

"Sure, that sounds great. Just order a ginger ale for me." This made me shutter inside. I felt like a cripple because I wasn't supposed to drink alcohol. I was sick of explaining that to every person with whom I socialized.

"So you never tied the knot, huh?" he said.

"No, I didn't and it kills me. I'd love to meet someone nice like you did. You are married and happy, aren't you?"

"Of course. I'm not so sure about the happy part. It's tough. I'm so dumb I married Nicole right out of dear old Holten High School."

"Didn't that scare you? Wasn't that too soon?"

"I didn't know any better."

"I wish I'd been that dumb."

"What do you mean?" Eddie said, giving me a puzzled look.

"I mean," I said, "why didn't I have the guts to get

married? I didn't have the guts to do anything right."

"I don't get you. I just don't understand. You had a lot of guts, for crying out loud. You played football and you stood up to Bruce Hatfield. You did a lot of brave things that I never done."

"All those moves were because of somebody else's advice. Remember my grandfather? It didn't take anything for me to do them. Jeez, I always turned to someone else for help."

Eddie gave me an odd look. "Ben, my buddy. You used to be such a great friend, my best friend, full of fun and everything. Now you don't seem so happy—you're down on yourself. C'mon, let's be buddies again and have a few laughs. I never had the chances you had. You must know that, don't you? I had two quick daughters, Debbie and Sheila, before I knew what time of day it was. C'mon! I was scared to death. I didn't even know if I could hack it. I had to work hard all my life."

"What're you trying to get at?" I said, concerned over his attitude. I'd never seen him in this light.

"Ben, you're a great guy—everyone dug you. I was always a clown. You know that. I never had the spunk you had. I got a brutal job lifting heavy stuff all day and then I have to go home at night and listen to my two girls' problems and God knows what else."

I sat there at the bar and began eating the hot pizza that had just been put in front of us. Just like he'd said, it was delicious. I looked around the whole place and saw something that was troubling to me. Half the men were so drunk it seemed as if they didn't know what they were doing or where they were. Some, I concluded, didn't belong in a bar in the first place. Perhaps they were just killing time by avoiding their families or something much worse.

"You know what I was just thinking?" I asked after gobbling down a slice of pizza. "I was thinking about Alice. What a beautiful girl she was. I was nuts over her, you know that? We were good for one another. What happened, anyway? I haven't seen her in years."

"You know me," he broke in. "Mr. know-it-all. I heard everything about Alice. I see Yvette a lot around Danvers and she told me that after Alice finished St. Jeans School For Girls she went to Emanuel College in Boston and got a degree in psychology, just like her mother. Remember her mother? She was real smart, just like Alice. Then Alice got married to a teacher from Maine and had a daughter. The last I heard she wasn't doing so good in her marriage. I haven't heard nothing more from Yvette since then."

"Wow, that's really awful. I can't believe it! If that's true, is there anyway I can get in touch with her?"

"No, I wouldn't do that. I don't know where she really lives, anyway, and if I did I don't think I'd tell you. It could be awful trouble for you. Maybe it's as bad as the Bruce Hatfield mess. You're dealing with a married couple here, buddy. She's no longer the innocent girl she was, you know."

"This never would've happened if I'd been a normal kid who wasn't so screwed up," I said, annoyed over the news. "If I'd gotten a good job after college and settled down,

I could've married her. Of course, who knows, my parents probably would've gone berserk because Alice is Catholic. It was always something with them. They only wanted me to go out with Protestant girls." I began laughing uncontrollably. "Eddie, you wouldn't have believed it even if you'd been there. Once a Jewish girl named Shirley Beth showed up at my house real late at night and my mother went ape. I'll never forget it." I started to cough because there was some pizza stuck in my throat.

"Where was your old man?"

"He wasn't around—someday I'll tell you about it."

Eddie shook his head and smiled. "Boy, you've really been through the ringer, huh?"

That was how our conversation went. If I'd learned anything from it, it was that everyone had tons of problems—not just me. I felt a tremendous burden being lifted from me that night. I always understood that life was complicated and crazy at times, but when Eddie Howard related his ups-and-downs to me, it struck home.

After our evening of chitchat and pizza at Louie's, I left hoping I'd see him again real soon.

CHAPTER THIRTY

It'd been almost three years since my father's death. My mother, the real warrior in the family, was still working in the Histology Laboratory at Salem Hospital. She'd had the job for over six years and had advanced to the position of supervisor of a department that was comprised of ten people. Her advancement hadn't surprised me at all. After all, she was smart and possessed excellent managerial skills besides being a go-getter. Her decision to acquire a job in the first place had been made for two reasons: she wanted to get out of the house and do something more constructive and challenging and my father had disappeared twice for long intervals in the course of their marriage. It had nothing to do with the fact that they didn't love one another. They surely did. Those two untimely events disrupted the general flow of our family. Adjustments had to be made. The first time Dad was missing for over a year. No one knew of his whereabouts. The Boston newspapers and television stations picked up on it. The Robblees were the center of attention in Danvers and around the North Shore. Some people, including myself, assumed that my father was dead. His white Continental, with most of his belongings intact, was found abandoned on Mystic River Bridge in Boston. There were no clues whatsoever as to what had caused his disappearance. It was true that his behavior, beginning months before, had been erratic at times. His moods had frequently changed. That had prompted my mother, who was always a strong person, to go to work. She'd had a couple of low-paying retail jobs before getting the one at Salem Hospital. In such a period of stress she'd been fortunate. A friend of one of her friends had known of the opening at the hospital. Her friend told her and she jumped at the opportunity. My mother began her new venture with a determined outlook as if her survival depended on her doing well. It did.

Because I'd always counted on Mom for a lot of things, there was no doubt that I took her for granted. And unlike in Dad's case when he was alive there wasn't any emotional obstacle I had to overcome to reach her. Everything between us was a natural, unbreakable process forged over the years.

A shocking moment materialized one morning just before she was heading out for work. On that particular occasion I noticed that something was dramatically different in her behavior. I instantly knew something was up, something perhaps life-changing. There was such a frightened look on my mother's face that I was taken back by its immediacy. I'd never had that feeling where she was concerned. She was on the verge of tears and simply said, "I have something to tell you, Ben. Please pay attention and listen."

I was finishing up my breakfast and murmured, "Sure, Mom."

"I'm very sick and I want you to understand what I'm about to tell you. It's serious and it's going to bother you, I'm sure." She was struggling with the right words to say.

"What do you mean?" I looked at her with an indescribable fear.

"I mean, sweetie, that I'm going to die. I have colon cancer and it's too advanced. The doctors have confirmed it. They can't do anything for me at this stage. So I've decided to allow the hospital to use whatever means are available to them. In a way, I'm going to be a guinea pig. Please don't be alarmed." She came over and hugged me tightly.

"Gee, Mom, I don't know what I'm going to do without you. Nothing can happen to you." A smattering of emotions came over me; I didn't know how to react.

"Yes, it can—and will. I'm going to die soon, Ben."

"Why are you going to work, then? Jeez."

"Because I have to do something, that's why. When it gets real bad, I'll go into the hospital and that will be it. You must be strong for me. You're going to have to get along without me. Do you understand?"

Late that same morning it finally hit me that my dear mother had a terminal case of cancer and she might live only another several months. I'd gone back to live with her during the last year. We were renting a small house at a reasonable rate in Ipswich, a small coastal town north of Danvers.

Water was nearby, all around the neck of the land, on the outskirts of town. It was like a small paradise. The sun gleamed off the ripples of water and seagulls were visible for miles. After thinking about it for a good long while, I was thankful that we were living by the sea. It was an appropriate place for my mother to spend her final days.

Before I'd gone back to live with Mom I'd shared an apartment with two guys. The three of us split the rent, thereby escaping any financial worries. I wasn't happy with that setup but I was forced to deal with it. One of my roommates was troubled. He had a severe drinking problem complicated by his addiction to gambling. That was a double whammy. His downfall was imminent unless he turned it around. He was agreeable only when he was sober, which was seldom.

The other fellow was so quiet that I never knew he was there unless I looked. His main interests included reading romance novels and watching soap operas on television. He was able to pursue those unusual interests because he had a night job. He was a bartender, a great one. His father, who'd divorced his mother when he was a toddler, was in the restaurant business. Even though he never realized it, he wanted to be like his Dad, though he hadn't seen him in many years. We were three young men who really belonged together; each of us was a genuine zero.

After several months of trying I'd finally gotten a job that, if not considered praiseworthy, was fairly secure. I was to be paid an hourly wage with benefits whereby, if I wanted to, I could rack up some decent overtime money. As usual I was to be at the very bottom of the totem pole, but it did make me feel better, boosted my confidence a little. Even though it wasn't anything I'd go around bragging about, I still was thankful for having found it. The job consisted of several duties, the major one being the daily sorting of hundreds of pieces of mail and then distributing them accordingly to the employees. I simply worked in the mail-room of an up-and-coming insurance company. It was a distribution center where thousands of units came in and went out on a daily basis. There was no doubt that I felt useful. If I could just keep my nose clean, it was possible that I'd keep the job for a long time. Of course that wasn't going to be easy for me to accomplish. The one big plus was that the company had a lot of friendly employees, especially beautiful women. They were everywhere to be seen. But I didn't really see how that benefited me. My love life, or lack of it, had never been anything to boast about. But I was a relatively young man who still had dreams, just an average guy who wanted eventually to find a nice woman to marry. I knew that was going to be difficult because I considered myself to be a mediocre person among the many millions of other mediocre people in the world. Yet I was hopeful and determined to change the course of my life.

My mother was rapidly losing her battle with cancer. It was sapping her strength day by day. I'd come home exhausted from my job and she'd be sitting in a beach chair on the porch overlooking the moody ocean. Being near the water had always been good for her; its mysterious vastness was a soothing force unlike any other. Like me she was a true romantic and also like me she'd suffered some things in silence.

It was the middle of July and, even in the extreme heat and humidity, she was wearing an overcoat to protect herself from the chilly breeze intermittently blowing in from the south. Brutus, one of our two dogs, was standing obediently on one side of the chair as if he were protecting her from the elements. ReRe, the female dog, was asleep on her other side. It was both a sad and beautiful scene to behold. It was as if my mother were gazing out toward the water and waiting to join my father in death. She was talking to the dogs as if they were real people who had the ability to understand her thoughts. I believed they did. At times either one of the dogs looked up at her as she rambled on. I never came close enough to her to comprehend what she was saying. I merely stood by the breezeway and studied my mother as she magically detached herself from the realities of life. There was no discernable fear whatsoever showing in her demeanor; whatever had been bothering her had vanished after she'd informed me of her illness. She already was at peace with herself. Infrequently she'd reached down to touch one of the dogs. This was far better for her than any medicine. Throughout her lifetime Grace Foster Robblee had often carried on conversations with her animals. She considered them superior to human beings. They'd always served her well in a time of need. In earlier days she'd had as many as fifteen cats. "Oh, Tinkerbell," she once whispered to a dying cat. "Don't worry, baby, you're going to be all right. Your mommy will see to it." She then kept kissing the poor thing, trying to coax the animal back to health. It was a sight that, if I weren't present, I never would've believed possible even if someone had told me. But I never said a thing to her about it because I respected Mom's right to carry on like that. She would've been devastated had I made fun of her. None of her cats was her favorite. Just as with her three sons, she was democratic in all her relationships. She seemed nevertheless to have a special love for Herman, a large overweight cat that she attended to constantly. "Now, Herman, stop eating so much, dear. You're going to blow up if you keep doing that." My patience was once severely tested when I awoke early one morning and discovered two cats staring at me from the bedpost. I almost said something to my mother about it, but at the last moment I decided not to complain. I knew that all the animals my mother kept in the house deeply unnerved my father. It distracted him mightily. Nonetheless, to my knowledge, he didn't let my mother know about his intense dissatisfaction. "Damn it," he complained to himself after nearly tripping over one of the creatures.

"The Cat Woman" some people called Mom when she wasn't around to hear them. I never knew whether that was a compliment or a criticism. She knew the names and habits of each cat. They had the capability of ridding her of all her stress and anger. She was widely known as a woman who carried her love of all creatures to an extreme. Without them she would've been a person without a soul; they were an integral part of her.

Toward the end of August my mother was admitted to Salem Hospital for the last time. Her farewell to Brutus and ReRe was a tear-filled event. It was as if both animals knew something was terribly wrong; they whined along with her.

Salem Hospital went out of its way by paying her several weeks of salary even though she hadn't been to work for a long while. It was a marvelous gesture on their part and she appreciated it. She was the type of person everyone wanted to help.

Before she left for the hospital we had several long conversations about my future. She was concerned, perhaps too much so, about my future happiness. She verbalized her strong doubts about me. How would I manage on my own? Would I ever find a suitable woman who'd be good for me? Was my job secure? By then I was forty-one years old. In essence, she was treating me like a fifth-grader, as if I were back at Port School. I was sure it was because I was still single, unlike my two brothers, and unsuccessful, also unlike Scott and Andy. I had the notion that most people viewed me negatively because I'd never really done much in my life to warrant their approval. I figured the higher the position a person held the more respect he was accorded.

My mother had always been aware of my constant headaches, dizzy spells, and irritating bouts of severe fatigue over the past twenty-four years. She refused to stop mentioning her anger, resentment, and deep disappointment over my football injury. She always understood that it'd greatly interfered with my general health and my chances for gainful employment, not to mention the fact my social life had suffered. And Mom considered my having played football a huge mistake, the biggest one in my life. But there was nothing she'd been able to do about it. Despite that, she always refused to mention my father as being the culprit responsible for that decision. How odd, I thought. She never owned up to it. That bothered me considerably. She looked upon my mishap in a more spiritual way. Was God punishing either her or me for something we'd done? I responded many times over that it'd just happened, that's all. The one certainty about our talks was that they weren't doing me any good at all. They were robbing me of my confidence. To keep going over and over the same nonsense wasn't solving a stupid thing. Forgive, accept, and move on had been the steadfast advice of my therapist. I hadn't done that yet. On and on it went.

I never informed my mother of the long-distance phone call I'd received one day from her cousin Rollene, who lived in Pasadena and had visited our family on a couple of occasions. The one thing I did remember about her the most was she'd been married three times and was very beautiful.

I certainly was very drawn to her. My mother confided in me that Rollene was attracted to men who had loads of money but were basically unkind to her. They unloaded their problems on her. She'd been abused many times and apparently couldn't help herself. Whenever a decent man had wanted her as his wife, she'd spurned him in favor of someone less suitable. In our lengthy conversation Rollene went on and on about my mother's love for me on the one hand and her serious concerns over my ability to fend for myself on the other. I failed to see how her revelation had a particularly uplifting affect on me. It did inspire me to wake up a bit and it definitely angered me. I knew that she was a lovely person and hadn't meant to hurt my feelings. Just maybe it'd been a scheme that she and my mother had concocted between the two of them.

Mom departed from this world on September 15, 1980. All those horrific months of suffering had finally ended. She was at rest and with the love of her life. My parents were reunited for the long haul. Scott had been the only one present when she'd passed away. He called me and simply uttered, "It's over," and hung up. On that morning I thought of the song my mother had always loved concerning her feelings for her second son. "To Know Him Is To Love Him," sung by "The Teddy Bears" in 1958, had been her favorite tune. I found it to be most appropriate at the moment I learned of her passing.

CHAPTER THIRTY-ONE

With my mother and father now gone, I was forced to look ahead and prove to myself instead of others that I was able to make it without the assistance of my parents. My obsession with what others thought of me had to cease. People I knew were always going to believe what they wanted to, anyway. I had to try not to pay heed to their nosiness plus I had to stop telling people my problems because they really didn't care a whit.

I had to rid myself of the bitterness I harbored toward the past. That horrible energy detracted from my going forward. I was still a relatively young man and it behooved me to face the future with a renewed optimism. That was all I could do even though it was going to be a difficult task to achieve.

About five months after my mother's death, something I didn't think possible happened. Maybe it was divine intervention, maybe not. While walking through the North Shore Shopping Center in Peabody for no apparent reason, I stopped at a coffee-and-doughnut shop. As I was standing there, I noticed a slender woman with a young girl at the register in front of me. I kept staring at her. I certainly believed I was wrong in who I thought it was.

After she'd been given her change, she turned around and saw me. Our eyes met for a few seconds. We both stood there, holding up the line of customers, and seemed unable to move.

It was definitely who I thought it was! It was Alice, that same wonderful girl who'd been my close friend at Port School. Only she was now a much older woman, but with the identical expressions she'd once had as a fifth-grader. She moved in the same graceful manner and her face, although featuring the signs of some wear, was striking but gave me the impression that she'd been burdened with much sadness in her heart. Her hair was now a reddish-blonde and combed back severely, unlike the innocent look of 1950. We approached each other cautiously. I wasn't able to speak for her, but I was so stunned I couldn't believe this was actually happening to me. It was as if I didn't really know what to say or do because I was afraid of her reaction to having run into me like this.

Thoughts of Port School sped through my mind. It was the exact feeling I'd had during that recess period thirty-one years ago. However, it was more intense and gave me a feeling of buoyancy, that all wasn't lost in my life. There she was! Even though she'd changed since she'd sat beside a dark-haired girl in the corner of Miss Potter's fifth-grade room, Alice possessed a more mature beauty. She was, however, thin and seemed to be very nervous, noticeably different from the past.

We embraced for several seconds. Then we looked at each other in disbelief. Without a doubt I hadn't had such a feeling as that in decades. It was something that, once I experienced it, couldn't be duplicated ever again. I absorbed this moment as if it were an elixir capable of changing my life. We stood in the same spot and talked for an hour or so before we went our separate ways.

EPILOGUE

I was going to see Alice that evening. She was divorced with a ten-year-old daughter named Samantha, a cute little redhead. She was back living with her parents in the same house near Eddie's old place—where we used to play records and eat her homemade chocolate chip cookies. I'd seen good old Eddie several times in the interim.

It was marvelous that I'd be retracing my steps by being with Alice after all those years. She told me at the shopping center that she was happy that we'd be together to go over old times. I was a bit edgy over our date and had mixed feelings. But my guess was that both of us had overcome obstacles that still had to be ironed out. It was much different than those exciting days at Port School. I certainly didn't know what to expect. Nor, I supposed, did she.

I was always stuck on Alice. I'd like to think that we were still attracted to one another. I was always comfortable around her, more so than with any other woman since then. Back in the early 50s things weren't the same. We were far more restricted then. That was a good thing. There were more rules to follow and people behaved better. Much later on it became more open. Mystery and innocence had vanished forever. That wasn't a good thing. I wished with all my heart and soul that I was able to return to the Truman-Eisenhower days when the little things in life meant something, when going to Ellison's for a candy bar or viewing black-and-white television was an anticipated treat. They existed no more!

Alice, as far as I was concerned, was still beautiful. Her sweet nature, I was positive, had been somewhat soured by her bad marriage. Those experiences along the path of life never were pleasant. I was going to try not to judge her, no matter what. Since people had judged me, I knew the score. I just wanted to be with her. And if I knew her at all, I was fairly sure she felt the same way. She always had been insightful, even at the tender age of eleven. She came from a supportive family that I firmly believed would be behind her through this difficult time.

I was well aware our meeting like that and the chance of our ever seeing each other again was a long shot. Hopefully our genuine fondness for one another would grow to mean more, but I wasn't counting on it. The way I saw it, there were no guarantees. However, for some reason I was very confident. I had to be optimistic and I prayed it was going to work out for us. I honestly didn't know how many more chances I'd have for happiness.

I'd take it easy and see what happened. If it was meant to be a close friendship, so be it. If it ended up being more, that would be even better. There was absolutely no pressure involved. Somehow I'd lost track of Alice after she'd entered parochial school in the seventh grade. Those things, unfortunately, occurred in life. Three decades had transpired just like that. Where had all those years gone? But just to see her expression of wonderment when we spotted each other at the donut shop had been worth the wait.

Ordinarily I wasn't a betting man but that one time I placed a wager we'd be seeing one another for quite some time. It was funny but I always knew that the Port was a special place that sparkled despite its reputation of being a little rough around the edges.

Louie's, the famous pizza joint where Eddie used to go to pick up his father at the bar, was still going strong. At that point, however, to keep up with the times it had added a lot to its menu. It seemed nothing in life was simple anymore. There was more of everything. I questioned whether that meant the world was a better place.

Perhaps Alice and I would go on our date that night to Louie's for a pizza. Then we'd walk around the old neighborhood like we used to do in the old days. Maybe we'd run into Eddie Howard and pretend we were back in the fifth grade at Port School. As if nothing had changed at all.

Printed in the United States
84665LV00009B/8/A